Silent Partner

The Sweet Version

Renee Vincent

writing as

Gracie Lee Rose

SILENT PARTNER (The Sweet Version)
Copyright © 2015, Renee Vincent writing as Gracie Lee Rose
Digital ISBN: 978-0-9855831-7-0
Trade Paperback ISBN: 978-0-9855831-6-3

Cover Art Design by Renee Vincent
Stock Art by BigStock.com
Editor, Linda Ingmanson

Digital Release, February, 2015
Trade Paperback Release, February, 2015

To God, for never leaving my side through this amazing journey. I am nothing without you.

****

To my fans, who continually make me smile with each new release. Your loyalty and dedication are why I do what I do. You make being an author the best job in the world. For you, I write.

ACKNOWLEDGEMENTS

To Kristen, for all your help and guidance concerning the hearing impaired and the deaf. You were a wealth of knowledge and I thank you for being there at my beck and call.

To Stephanie, for giving me a glimpse into the heart and mind of the deaf. It was an absolute honor to speak with you and get to know you as a person. I will never forget how your words have touched me.

To my cousin, Kelli, for taking the time out of your busy schedule and helping me to find the perfect home for my hero and heroine. One day, I hope to visit you in the historic Back Bay in Boston and stand in the places my characters frequented.

And finally, to my husband, Gregory. You are my rock. "You and me."

SILENT PARTNER (The Sweet Version)

Grayson Anders has it all. He's the co-owner of a happening nightclub in downtown Boston, he's wealthy, and women can't resist him. But he doesn't want just any woman. His passion is dancing and he's determined to find the perfect dance partner.

Chloe LaRoche is a talented artist, but a failing entrepreneur. Her once thriving studio is now on the brink of foreclosure and unless she paints the next Van Gogh Starry Night, she'll have to cut her losses and say goodbye to her quaint little gallery. Fearing her career is at an end, she drags herself to the local hot spot, fixed on drowning her worries in the bottom of a shot glass...until she lays eyes on the wickedly sexy, swarthy dancer in the club—Grayson Anders.

Unable to resist, Chloe finds herself in Grayson's arms, indulging in a passionate, one night stand. And when they awaken the next morning, they're both consumed with inspiration. Grayson finds his perfect dance partner and Chloe discovers her muse. But will her secret destroy both their dreams?

Chapter One

There he was.

Shaking his cute little bum on the dance floor of Gyrations, the hippest nightclub in downtown Boston, amid a flock of beautiful women.

Chloe had first noticed him chatting with the bartender when she entered the strobe-lit room and wandered up to the bar. Their discussion looked important as they hovered over a business calendar. But once a change of song had happened, he dismissed himself from the conversation with a purposeful expression, and headed straight for the dancefloor—probably hoping to score.

She couldn't tell which of the loose women he was looking to get lucky with as there were so many dancing around him. Their barely there clothes shimmered beneath the illuminating black light as each one competed for his attention. She didn't blame them. He was quite possibly the sexiest man she'd ever seen.

He wore sleek black painted-on leather pants, a tight white tank, and a have-your-fill-of-me grin on his handsome face. He seemed to enjoy himself as he moved to the beat of the booming bass, and his hips looked as if they were dislocated from the rest of him.

Oh, he knew how to dance—quite well—and he wasn't afraid to show it among the many who were crammed into the joint. In fact, he held many people's attention—not just hers—as if he had a reputation to live up to. As if the prize for "best male dancer" was up for grabs.

She didn't think there was such an event going on at the crowded nightspot, but she would definitely cast her vote in his favor if there was. No one in the place could even come close to matching his abilities. His steps were graceful, his rhythm was spot-on, and his lithe, muscular body moved in ways she didn't think possible. His hips entranced every female in the club, and probably infuriated every male who was left holding up the bar.

Chloe gazed around the trendy, atmospheric room and took in the many aggrieved faces of the men standing in random corners. She assumed they were all either watching Casanova in hopes of learning something, or waiting for him to make a move on their girlfriends just so they could have a reason to vent their jealousies.

As she glanced back at Mr. Gyration, he was now grinding against some blonde's tight-jeaned derriere, his hands on her hips. She noticed the women's expressive face, her lips parted and her eyes half-closed. It was obvious she enjoyed the suggestive dance way too much.

Chloe sighed and looked away, tossing back a shot of tequila. She knew the only way she was going to get lucky tonight was if she awoke tomorrow morning without a horrendous hangover. At this point in the game, she didn't look beyond her next shot and let the burn of the alcohol soothe her troubled mind.

She was two drinks in and raised her hand for another.

The bartender, cool and confident, opened the broad-bottomed bottle of Patrón and leaned toward her, his weight casually resting on one elbow. "You sure 'bout this, honey?"

Of course, she was sure. She wouldn't have ordered it to begin with had she been apprehensive about the drink's potential. She knew well what the hard liquor could do and had high hopes it would soon help her to forget her worries.

She was an artist—a starving artist. If she didn't find a way to sell more of her paintings, she was going to lose everything. Her shop. Her home. Her life.

Every little bit of her savings had gone toward the funding of her big dream. And for a while, things had looked promising. Her paintings were moving out the door on a fairly regular basis. Her biggest clients had been young, wealthy doctors and lawyers who aimed to spruce up their penthouse bachelor pads with risqué nudity in an artistic form. On occasion, she'd even locked in a few hairdressers who wanted the more tasteful pieces for their salons.

But those avenues had soon run dry.

Word of mouth had gone only so far, and with the changing economy, no one was willing to spend their hard-earned money on needless fine art. If she didn't figure out a way to stimulate the public's senses enough to open their wallets, she would have to give up her small independent business and kiss her entrepreneurial life good-bye.

With a flip of her hand, she gestured for the concerned bartender to pour another shot, fixed on the goal of drinking away her problems.

"This may look like water, darlin', and go down just as smooth, but it ain't so easy on the head." He looked her over as if measuring her determination, and after a few seconds, he popped the cork-lined glass top. "What do I care, huh? As long as you're paying…"

Feeling something brush against her arm, Chloe looked to her left. To her surprise, it was Mr. Gyration, flipping a twenty on the bar.

"You shouldn't care at all, Jack," he said. "Especially if I'm footing the bill. And make that two."

Her stomach fluttered. Being on the receiving end of

that cocky smile did a number on her heart. As her breath staggered out of her, all she could do was smile in return.

She glanced at the crisp Jackson resting next to her shot glass, appreciative of Mr. Gyration's generosity. At least he tried to be a gentleman, which was completely opposite the impression he'd made on the dance floor. She could only hope he'd continue to be that way, for she had no intention of tolerating anything less.

"You're a pretty little thing," he said, leaning against the bar. "A girl like you shouldn't be anywhere alone. Especially here."

Jack slammed two shots of tequila on the slick, lacquered wood of the bar. "Easy, Don Juan. She's new."

"I can see that."

His devilish smile was too much to handle, and Chloe had to look away. Even though a warning had slipped from the bartender's lips, Mr. Gyration didn't seem to care. He stared at her with such hunger, she half expected him to growl like an animal.

Trying to shrug off the weight of his proximity, she reached for the alcohol, dying to douse the flame of his dark-amber eyes from her memory. But his hand stopped her.

His abrupt action caused the drink to slosh and splash her fingers. She barely noticed. All she could feel were his masculine fingers curling gently around her wrist. The warmth of his palm, flattened across her forearm, spread like wildfire throughout her body. The shock of his touch nearly stopped her heart. What stunned her more was watching him lift her hand and take her wet finger into his mouth to suck the small droplets of tequila from it.

Her stomach dropped to her pelvis, and a tingling sensation of chills danced across her skin. Though his tongue only swirled around her knuckle, she could feel its torment everywhere.

She crossed her legs, trying to get a grip on her emotions, trying to keep him from weaseling into her good sense. But the way he withdrew her finger ever so slowly from his soft, full lips clouded her brain. His inviting golden-brown eyes blurred everything around her.

No one existed save him.

"Let's dance first," he suggested coolly. "Then we can shoot the good stuff together."

Chloe didn't have the opportunity to refuse. He'd already pulled her from her seat and was leading her into the thick of the crowded dance floor.

Her feet faltered and her legs wobbled, almost as if they'd lost all circulation. His grip on her hand was strong, domineering. She knew there was no pulling free. He was a very determined man, and if she happened to slip from his grasp, he'd only pursue her.

She looked around, taking in all the people who checked her out as she passed by. Most were jealous looks from women—regular club-hoppers, disappointed that Mr. Gyration hadn't chosen them as his partner.

Chosen.

It seemed like such a stupid concept given the countless options he had in this meat-market. She could only wonder why he'd opted for her.

She wasn't a loose woman. Anyone could see that simply by her choice of attire. She was dressed in a modest denim skirt—nowhere near as short as what the other girls in the place wore—and her blouse was silky, buttoned up to the top. Not a hint of cleavage to be seen. Yet, as he found an open spot on the floor and turned, his gaze poured over her as if her clothes weren't even there.

He jerked her into his arms, and she slammed into the solid wall of his chest. He smiled coyly. "Hold on tight, sweet thing," he said as he snatched her other hand, establishing a strong frame between them. "I'm about to sweep you right off your feet."

He wasn't lying.

His forearm tightened on her lower back, and he swung her around in a quick spin, his hips never breaking contact with hers. She was lost in his gaze while the commanding force of his arm held her attention more than the flashing lights and the crazy club atmosphere around her.

Though the loud bass vibrated against her, helping her to judge when to step into him and when to withdraw, she was oblivious to everything else. His lean, hard muscles felt good against her as he guided her into the next steps of their dance.

She knew her way around a closed dance position, each of their movements mirroring the advancement and withdrawal of an equal and opposite step. He was skilled enough in his timing and technique that anyone paired up with him would look like a professional.

He slipped his arm from around her back and threw her to the side, holding her hand as she spun away from him. With their arms extended to the fullest, she looked back at him, and he smiled, showing his immense delight before he tugged her back into his embrace.

They locked hands again, and he stepped into her, his pelvis jutting forward. Together, they stepped across the floor and carved a wide circle within the tight group of dancers, opening their space. Everyone obliged, though they didn't do so happily.

Sneers from envious women flashed in Chloe's direction. She was enveloped in the arms of a highly prized man, and no one but she was having the chance to partake in such a pleasure.

At least not tonight.

Though she knew he was only toying with her emotions and trying to see how far he could get with her, she put her cynical thoughts aside and decided to indulge in this one delight.

Not often would a wickedly sexy man pick her out of a crowd and dance with her as though he had yearned for this chance all night, especially when there were more promising choices at his disposal. But his intense expression said he didn't give a damn about his other options. He was with her, and that was all he seemed to care about at the moment.

Through the rest of the dance, his gaze never wavered. If anything, she saw a deeper longing in his tawny, seductive eyes, an amber glow of fire burning into her. It spread across every inch of her, smoldering in places where his touch lingered.

The palms of her hands.

The small of her back.

The sensitive area of her pelvis crushed against his.

He was a tango tornado as he spiraled her out of his arms, and back again, only to dip her over his forearm. As he dragged his free palm down her neck and between her breasts, his thumb and pinky brushed over her chest through her blouse.

Chloe blushed as if every drop of her blood had pushed its way through the narrow veins of her neck and flooded her face. She was shocked, to say the least, but knowing a typical tango maneuver and personally experiencing it were two different things. In all honesty, she wanted him to do it again. She wanted to feel his hands all over her. And not just a slight brush of his fingertips as before, but a heavy spread of masculine hands stroking her hungry flesh.

He had ignored her look of disbelief and jerked her closer by her waistband, enveloping her with a formidable embrace around her back. She glanced down at the dark-complexioned hand still gripping her denim skirt. The hard knuckles of his fingers pressed temptingly against the soft skin of her stomach. He tormented her. Easily. And he knew it.

Crap, it's hot in here.

For a moment, she started to blame the amount of alcohol she'd consumed, but once his fingers moved slightly across her skin, she quickly reneged on that theory. It was more likely due to the practiced man who touched her and stared at her with insatiable lust, which was by no means unfavorable. He was gorgeous, and the only thing she could think of was how beautiful he must be when stripped of his clothing.

She imagined he was like a Greek statue—a modern-day Adonis—chiseled, hard, and stunningly streamlined. Every part of him was straight out of an Acropolis Museum exhibit, from the beauty of his unforgettably handsome face to the perfection of his male physique. He actually made her want to try her hand at sculpting clay instead of painting.

She had never sculpted before, but it was easy to envision her hands molding over his chest and arms, kneading and shaping every bulge on his torso. She even dared to think of her hands forming the tight orbs of his cute little butt. How she'd enjoy spending time casting his entire physique with precision, down to the finest detail of his supple lips and the slight shadow of facial hair framing them.

Chloe found herself staring at his well-groomed goatee. His thin, dark mustache accentuated his full, luscious lips, while the vertical strip of hair from his lower lip drew her attention toward his strong chin and jaw.

She assumed he spent a lot of time trimming his beard because it was a part of him he wanted women to notice.

I noticed, all right.

His mouth was so alluring, so inviting, so…coming

closer!

Automatically, she drew back and stiffened.

"What's wrong?" he asked. "Not into public displays of affection?"

She'd come here intending to forget her troubles. And letting Mr. Gyration kiss her would no doubt erase all memory of that. And then some.

Hell, he was making her forget things now.

She shouldn't get caught up in this player because, frankly, that was all he was. She'd be nothing to him but another oat sowed, a tally on his board, a number on his scorecard…and come morning, he'd never think twice about her.

Despite the fact that those piled-high reasons hadn't come close to meeting the height of her curiosity, she wanted his affection more than anything, publicly displayed or not. More than another shot of Patrón. More than trying to figure out a way to save her business.

He moved into her, backing her up until she hit the wall behind her. "I'm with you on the no PDA thing," he muttered. "Because once I kiss you, I'm not going to stop, and no one here wants to see that."

Chapter Two

Did he really just say that?

A red flag flew up, and Chloe swallowed hard, replaying his words. She didn't have time to process it, for he leaned his head toward hers, letting his nose nudge her cheek as he took in a long breath.

He pulled back. "Wait here. We forgot something."

As he left her standing in the dark corner of the club, she couldn't agree more. They had both forgotten something, all right—their self-control.

When it came to Mr. Gyration, she didn't know enough about him to assume anything about his reserve. Judging by the way he was with the other women in the place, she doubted he knew what that particular word meant.

She searched the dance floor, looking for a reason to turn him down. It would have to be a big reason, knowing how badly she wanted to take him up on his offer. Perhaps an unhappy girlfriend left dancing alone, or that one blonde floozy who'd have good cause to raise a stink about her being with him. But no one seemed to fit those criteria.

It was as if no one even knew she was there, waiting. Waiting for Mr. Gyration to return to her and take her somewhere private to...

What the hell am I doing?

She had to leave. There was no way around it. She had to escape the club or she was sure to get herself into something she'd regret. And if she left now, she'd walk away with her heart unscathed and her dignity intact.

Yes. Leaving him behind was her best option.

She closed her eyes, trying to convince herself that she didn't need the dark, sexy stranger's kiss.

Who was she kidding? Unless the hefty bald bouncer came over and dragged her out of the club, she wasn't going to budge.

"Ready to steal away to my humble abode?"

Chloe's eyes flashed open to find Mr. Gyration but a few inches from her, holding two full shot glasses—the ones they had left at the bar. He stepped forward. "You'll have to snag the keys out of my right pocket if you want that privacy," he suggested, glancing downward. "I'd do it myself, but my hands are full."

Come on, Chloe... Where's your sense of adventure? Reach into his tight leather pants and pull out his keys.

She took a deep breath and hesitated as her fingertips

breached the open seam of his pocket. She couldn't look at his face knowing he probably sported that half-cocked grin that made her blush like a teen girl with a crush. Somehow, she found the courage to reach inside and fish for his keys, but the close-fitting leather fabric of his pants made it difficult for her not to graze him repeatedly in the process.

"You're killing me, darlin'."

And I'm dying of humiliation. May I suggest a baggier pair of pants next time? Finally, she drew the ring of keys from his pocket and held them up like a prize.

He stepped back and gestured with his eyes to a narrow corridor behind her to the right. "After you."

With the keys to paradise in her hand, she slipped past him and started down the hallway, her knees shaking as she walked. They passed a couple who obviously had no qualms about a public display of affection, kissing passionately against the wall. Her mind ran wild and visions of a secret room that only VIP members could access popped up. A swingers club.

She'd heard of places like that, but it wasn't what she had in mind. She turned around, definite in her decision that she was not going to partake in anything that required a consent form.

Mr. Gyration ignored her sudden change of heart and backed her against the very door in question, bracing his drink-filled hands on either side of her. She should have felt trapped, scared. But it was the way he looked at her that left her at ease. His gaze fell over her as though he had never seen a more beautiful woman in his life and he was not about to share her with anyone.

She closed her eyes as he tucked his face beneath her jaw. His lips barely brushed her neck as he whispered something. His warm breath bathed her skin, but she had no idea what he said. All she could hear was the pounding of her own heart in her ears.

His exquisite mouth suckled her sensitive neck with a practiced kiss, weakening her with every tender flick of his tongue. She needed him. Needed his love, if only for one night. And what would it hurt to succumb to this extraordinary moment, this once-in-a-lifetime opportunity to be in the arms of a much-desired man?

She deserved it. She'd worked her whole life trying to be successful, trying to be prized and unique in the competitive world of art. For once, she felt special, as if she were the only woman he craved and no other woman in the universe would do.

As if he sensed her hesitation, he pulled away. "I'm not going to hurt you, and I'm not going to force you upstairs to my apartment. You decide. Right here. Right now. But once you unlock this door…you're mine. All night long."

Apartment?

His apartment.

All night long…

Okay, that was the answer she needed. Beyond this door was not a passage to someplace scandalous. He was inviting her to his private home.

Above a dance club, though?

"I own the building," he said, giving her more encouragement. "My apartment is up two flights to the left. So, what'll it be?" He rocked his sexy, leather-clad hips to the background beat of the DJ's music, his stunning amber eyes boring into hers.

All night long…

His words echoed in her head. The thought of having him all to herself until the sun came up made her choice easy. She held up the keys, indicating she didn't know which was the magic one. He pointed to the shiny silver one without spilling a drop of tequila. "And then you'll need the one behind it for upstairs."

Oh boy… She was really doing this.

Spinning on her heels, she faced the exit door. She squeezed her eyes shut and made faces as she came to terms with it. She never realized how hard inserting a simple key into a door could be until this moment. Her hands shook and the damn slot seemed to shrink as she tried three times to line it up.

Mr. Gyration didn't help matters either. She could feel the tickle of his breath in her hair, but his whispered words fell upon deaf ears as she tried to block out the sweet agony of him encroaching upon her space.

Finally, the key slid all the way in, and she pushed the door open. She didn't have to look to see if he followed. She sensed his looming presence behind her. But she stopped abruptly.

This was her last chance to make sure she really wanted to do this. To indulge in this one-night stand without regret.

Chloe turned and faced him, glancing toward his tempting lips. The look of them, soft and supple, wasn't enough. There was no way to know how wonderful his kisses would be without actually trying them. She clasped his face in her hands and stood on her tiptoes, leaning forward.

Surprisingly, he stood very still, letting her lips meet his. The rugged male scent of his skin combined with the slight fragrance of his expensive cologne clouded all rational thought, and the soft prickle of his goatee erased all prudence.

As she kissed him, his mouth opened slightly and his tongue brushed over her lower lip, patiently, as if he had no

Renee Vincent writing as Gracie Lee Rose

intention of rushing through her little experiment. She touched the tip of her tongue to his, testing him, tasting him. The sheer delight of it all twisted her body into knots.

She wanted more.

Angling her face, she gave him all the leeway he needed to kiss her in the way he wanted—the way she'd yearned for since the moment he'd sucked the tequila from her finger.

He didn't disappoint. He showed her just how well his tongue could feel twisting with hers, and her knees nearly buckled.

When she faltered, he pulled back, breathing hard. "Switch with me. I need my hands."

Though confused by his demand, she took the two glasses from his possession, and he in turn retrieved the keys from her grasp.

"Don't spill 'em," he warned as he picked her up and wrapped her legs around his waist. With the correct key ready to insert in the next door, he swiftly carried her up the flight of stairs and sought to kiss her again.

He never missed a beat. From his able stair-stepping footwork to the skillful play of his tongue, he was both patient and passionate, explorative and precise. She'd never been kissed this way. All the way up the stairs, he held her as if she were a precious jewel, his arms solid and

27

unyielding.

How many more steps already!

His momentum finally broke, and his right arm shifted, only long enough to insert the next key in the door, and then his mouth was back on hers. Clumsily, he turned the handle and kicked the door open wide, then carried her through.

A few more long strides, and they were at his apartment door. He fumbled blindly for the third key. With her still in his arms and his face buried in a kiss, it made for a difficult task.

He growled an indeterminable slew of words and set her on her feet. Sandwiched between the cool face of the door and his sizzling warmth, she watched him frantically flip through the keys. Even in his agitated state, he was exceptionally handsome in the dark shadows of the hallway.

After one more curse, he found the right one and shoved it into the lock. A slow, wide smile spread across his face as he pushed the door open from behind her. He bent to steal another kiss and backed her inside, then dropped the keys on the floor.

Tangled up in each other's arms, they couldn't get close enough. Even when he threw his hands behind his shoulders and ripped his tank over his head, she couldn't satisfy the ache that begged her to throw the shot glasses aside and take him in her own hands. To knead his brawny chest and arms...

"I don't know what I was thinking," he spat as he snatched the drinks from her and chucked them over his shoulder. "Drinking is the furthest thing from my mind right now."

Still in awe that he'd actually tossed them, she peered around him in the dark, looking for the mess, expecting to see glass all over his beautiful hardwood floor.

He caught her face. "Forget it. I'll clean it up later."

His fingertips blazed a trail to her shoulders and across her clavicles, opening the collar of her blouse. Immediately, he bent to kiss her there, his lips brushing over her now goose-pimpled flesh.

Oh, he was so damn good at foreplay that she could hardly brace herself for what was to come. He pulled her from the wall and steered her through the maze of furniture in his spacious living room, down the hall to his bedroom. Ready or not, he was going to strip away her clothes, piece by piece, and have his way with her.

...all night long.

She wasn't used to having casual sex. For her, sex came with commitment, with emotions, with love. And though she hadn't had many partners in the past, she could at least say those few encounters involved some sort of deep connection before sex came into play.

Here, with this man, there was nothing but carnal lust.

They didn't know each other outside the club, nor did they even know each other's names. Given time, she could probably fall madly in love with the guy. But when it came to having spontaneous sex with him, she wondered if he'd even remember her in the morning. If she would ever cross his mind again.

Don't complicate it, Chloe.

Yeah, that was what she was doing. And heaven knew she didn't need any more complications in her life. This was supposed to be a moment to indulge herself. To forget her problems for one night and live it up. To have nothing but no-strings-attached, wild sex with a man hardly worth resisting. Hardly worth regretting come sunup.

Intent on moving forward, she reached to unbutton his fly. His eyes flew open. "You're certainly full of surprises tonight, sweet thing. You…sitting at the bar like a spectator, looking out into the crowd like you wished you could dance. When all along, you knew exactly how." His gaze fell over her, from head to toe, and back up again. "Then you hide all this beneath a straitlaced silk blouse and denim skirt. Who would've guessed?"

Chloe swallowed hard.

He furrowed his brow, eyeing her differently now.

"Not much for talking, are you?"

Her heart skipped. Maybe she wasn't cut out for this casual-sex thing after all.

"Okay, I get it," he replied with a wink. "Sex now...talk later. That's fine by me." He kicked out of his shoes and pants and hoisted her up by her bottom. In one swift move, they fell together onto the bed and landed precisely in a missionary position. The weight of his body held her firmly against his soft pillow-top mattress as she caught her breath.

If anything, she was thankful to be lying down, for his devious grin would've knocked her on her backside anyway. He was the devil himself disguised as Adonis, both of whom he'd give a good run for their money.

He took her lips, but this time his kiss wasn't as wild and hasty as when he'd thrown her to the bed. He did wicked things to her soul, charming her into the temptress she never believed she could be. She enjoyed being brazen. Bold. And naughty in this man's bed.

It was downright sinful to make love to a man for no other reason than just because. As far as she was concerned, she didn't need to have a reason. Being within his arms, beneath his perfect body, was motive enough.

She felt cherished, as if she was the only woman he had ever wanted to lie with.

Surely, she knew better, as he wasn't the kind of man who'd turn women away. He wasn't so humble in that respect. But he was a man who knew how to make a sensible woman question her own intuition. To strip her of any reserve she might have and all self-conscious thought.

For Chloe, that was all she'd aimed to do this night. And ignoring her common sense wouldn't result in a painful hangover. The only part of her she could imagine hurting might be her pride, and she could live with that. Considering her prized canvases were on display for all the bitter critics of the world on a daily basis, she knew how to swallow it.

Chapter Three

Chloe's internal alarm clock went off, and she opened her eyes. The dim light of dawn barely broke through the third-story window. Realizing the window treatments were unfamiliar—practically bare compared to the thick, opaque, Renaissance-style draperies shrouding her windows—she glanced around the room in a panic.

No, Chloe…you aren't dreaming. You spent the night with Mr. Gyration last night, and it's now the next morning.

She swallowed. Hard.

This was what that awkward moment of the morning-after felt like. Not only did the sun shed its light upon the discarded articles of clothing strewn around the room, it also illuminated how rash their actions had been from the night before.

She glanced beside her, getting one last look at the man who had bewitched her into his bed. His expression was almost angelic but no less masculine as he slept. He lay flat on his stomach with his long, heavy arm draped across her waist. The dark complexion of his bare back and limbs was a striking contrast to the soft yellow Egyptian cotton sheets tangled around his lower half. The sharpness of his chiseled face against the delicate contours of the pillow were so distinct, she couldn't help but think a genuine Hellenistic sculptor would have a field day recreating him.

How was she going to wiggle out from underneath his arm without waking him? She had no idea what kind of sleeper he was, whether he could snooze through a bomb detonation or if he'd awaken at the sound of a pin dropping.

Yeah, this was why she didn't do casual sex.

These were the types of things a person should know about their consensual partner before jumping into bed. Call it an unwritten rule, but she always liked to at least know what a man's favorite color was, or if he were a vegetarian, or the name of his best friend. With this guy, she knew nothing of the sort.

Hell, she didn't even know his name.

She'd overlooked both a simple customary greeting and her own unwritten rules as if they never existed, all because of one man's intense look. One man's talented hips and hands, and his ability to charm himself into her pants.

She closed her eyes, fighting back the urge to cast this amazing one-night-stand into the pile of terrible mistakes she'd made in her life. Sure, it was probably not the best decision she'd ever made, but she certainly didn't want to start regretting it. He was too good to regret. Too incredible to shove into a stockpile of loser boyfriends. Quite frankly, he was too gorgeous *not* to brag about—even if she only boasted of him to a few close friends.

He'd chosen her out of all those available women and was now lying facedown. Naked. With his arm around her—her!

That alone was brag worthy.

With a smile, she refused to regret last night's encounter and decided to chalk it up as a night she'd never forget.

Think of things you do know about him, Chloe. Those intimate things…

Unable to help herself, she gave in to that wicked inner voice and brought to mind his lower abdominals, how they formed an unmistakable "V" below his navel. She remembered how amazing his toned body felt beneath her touch, the velvety smoothness of his skin over hard planes of muscle.

Not long after that magnificent recollection, her practical inner voice spoke out as well.

What are you doing? Quit wasting time. Get the hell out before he wakes up and you're obliged to explain your pitiful life story. He's not going to care, and you'll only make things awkward. Get out now, while you still have these blissful memories to savor.

With a sigh, Chloe slowly turned her head and peered over the side of the bed. She saw her heels, her light-blue thong and matching bra lying on the shiny hardwood floor, and, contrary to her guarded subconscious, she recalled how they had ended up there.

A rush of warmth infused her cheeks as she thought about his hands, particularly adept in clothing removal, and how they'd also stripped her of modesty. She couldn't help it. Those were some of the best memories she'd ever remember, and if she wanted to rehash them, then darn it, she had every right. This was no average Joe lying naked beside her. This was Adonis, reincarnated in human form, and he—*Oh God!*—just moved.

His large, masculine hand slid absently up her torso. She held still, frozen as he rolled up on his side and discovered her bare breast in the process, cupping her. He seemed to be content with his find and fell back into a deep slumber.

Once she saw the rise and fall of his shoulders, she was finally able to breathe herself. However, she was in a no less worse situation given the new placement of his hand.

Cursing inwardly, she slid toward the edge of the bed, watching his limp hand drag across her chest until it dropped onto the mattress. Her gaze flashed up at his face.

Thankfully, he didn't stir, or notice that her body heat had been replaced by the flat coolness of the sheets.

She certainly did.

As she stood beside the bed, looking down at him, the sensation of his touch lingered on her skin. And damn if she didn't want to leap back in bed with him.

No, she heard a voice say. *You'll only ruin this moment. Instead...capture it.*

Like a light flicking on, an idea broke free from the confines of her shadow-dampened muse. She might not be a Greek sculptor, but that didn't mean she couldn't create something as dramatic and detailed as the famous *Drunken Satyr* using her oils.

Inspired by the simple beauty of this man lying in his expensive bed, she bent to pick up her clothes and heels, her creative juices flowing over long strokes of color and contrast. With nothing on her mind but bringing this perfectly serene moment to life, she tiptoed out of the bedroom.

****

Grayson opened his eyes, smiling as he remembered the beautiful woman who had danced with him last night—and shared his bed. A vision of how stunning she looked and how gracefully she moved played over in his head. But it vanished the moment he reached out and felt nothing but an empty space beside him.

Confused, he sat up, looking around his sunlit bedroom. The only evidence of her ever being there was the impression still left behind on his pillow. He opened his mouth to call out for her, and then closed it again.

He didn't know her name.

After realizing they'd never properly introduced each other, he slumped back down in his bed, disappointed, and planted his nose in the pillow upon which she had slept. A hint of her fragrance filled his senses, and he smiled again, recalling the sweet vanilla aroma of her skin, the delicate softness of her curves as he'd removed her clothes last night, piece by piece. And to think all that feminine sumptuousness had been hidden from every man's eyes, save his. By her style of dress, no one could have known the sexy temptress beneath all that fabric, and it seemed to be one of the reasons he liked her so much.

She was unlike other women he'd met. She wasn't caught up in how she looked or how to desperately appeal to the opposite sex. And she didn't seem hell-bent on hooking a man's attention by flashing generous amounts of skin.

Her skirt was tight but long. Below her knees. The type

of skirt a woman could wear to a family function.

His thoughts ran wild over their passionate sexual encounter, and he couldn't forget the dainty baby-blue intimate apparel he'd discovered when he'd removed her refined attire. Her sheer, lacy undergarments were definitely not family functional.

He sighed, rolling to his back, and took the sweet-smelling pillow with him. With his arms wrapped around it, he drew in a long breath, imagining her still in his embrace.

He liked that image—too much—and many times throughout last night, he'd been hard put to hide his delight. The pleasure she'd afforded him was priceless, for no one had ever been able to satisfy him like she had.

And yet, he didn't know her name.

Arising in a flash, he threw his legs over the side of the bed, determined to find the elusive woman who had so impressed him. He rushed to his dresser drawer and snatched a pair of jeans. As he pulled them on, he hobbled out of his room and into the hallway, practically tripping as he dressed. Jerking on the zipper, he stopped. The sight of his living room doorway—where he had chucked two full shot glasses—shocked him.

His hardwood floor, where he had expected to see a mess of shattered glass and puddled alcohol, was completely clean. Not a shred of last night's carelessness could be found.

He smiled. *She's a clean freak...*

Perfect. Because he was too.

If he'd learned anything from his mother, it was the importance of cleanliness and organization. There was nothing he hated more than inefficiency.

Still doubting she'd actually taken the initiative to clean up his mess before she left, he padded to the kitchen and jerked open the pantry door. Leaning against the doorframe, he shook his head upon seeing the shards of glass in the shiny metal waste can.

Unbelievable...

For the first time in his life, he found himself flirting with the idea of keeping a woman around. He was an only child, and having someone else in the picture to complicate his self-indulgent lifestyle—or hamper it, as he often saw it—was not something he cared to consider. All too often, women wanted him for two things: his money and bragging rights for being Grayson Anders's love interest. Neither of which he was willing to offer. Sure, some were worth bedding a time or two, but aside from that, most lingered far too long for his taste. So much so that he'd quit pursuing the opposite sex as readily as he had in his younger years.

But as he considered the woman from last night, he

found himself longing to be with her. He had to admit, she was too good to be true. She could dance like no other woman he'd ever seen, and she had the power to charm him into a relationship. The thought of one, anyway.

What puzzled him most was that she hadn't waited around to find out if a relationship was in the works. Hell, she hadn't even stayed long enough to say good-bye. Had it not been for the broken glass in his garbage, he would've sworn he'd dreamed her. That he'd concocted the perfect woman in his wild imagination.

A knock at the door broke into his reverie. For a split second, his heart leapt.

Had she come back? Was she not able to stay away from him any longer than he could from her?

Elated to find out, he ran to the foyer, his bare feet almost slipping out from underneath him as he turned the corner. Grabbing the handle, he threw open the door with a huge smile.

"Oh," Grayson mumbled upon seeing his friend Richard, dressed in the usual suit and tie. "It's just you. Come on in."

"Nice to see you too, Gray."

Grayson turned on his heel to hide his rolling eyes as he wandered into his living room. He plopped on his couch, running his hands down his face. "Is this going to take long? I've got some place to be."

"Dressed like that?" Richard asked. "Doubt you'll get very far unless you've taken up exotic dancing now."

Grayson glanced down at his bare chest and half-opened fly. Grimacing, he zipped his jeans. "What do you want?"

Richard strolled into the room, paused at the other sofa across from Grayson, and sat down just as purposefully. There was a certain air of cautiousness in the way Richard unbuttoned his Italian suit coat before sitting, almost as if he were about to address a panel of uptight board members from his downtown artist cooperative, R. Fitzgerald Gallery.

"What's up, Richard?"

His friend took a deep breath and smoothed his tie. "We have to move forward."

Grayson drew back. "All right. But don't I at least deserve dinner and a movie first?"

Richard sighed. "I'm serious, Gray. I agreed to take on this dance club and studio as your friend, but I'm speaking to you as a co-owner. We've been open now for more than five months, and the studio has lagged behind. I know you're searching for that perfect female partner but—"

"Richard, I've—"

"Dammit, Gray, let me finish."

Grayson threw up his hands, giving his friend the floor. "Have at it."

"Thank you. As I was saying, I know you don't want to open the studio until you find your dance partner, but we need someone by the end of next month. I have contractors coming in this afternoon to renovate, and that's that. I don't like pushing you or stepping on your toes, you know that. But this is a business arrangement, and banks don't give a shit about your perfect partner. They want payments at regular intervals, and we don't have the budget for putting this off any longer. We barely have enough for the labor. There. I said my piece."

Grayson laughed at Richard's tirade and headed toward the kitchen. "You want a drink?" he asked.

"No, I do not." Richard followed him into the kitchen as Grayson pulled an Evian out of the fridge. He leaned across the marble countertop. "I want an answer from you. I want an 'Okay, Richard, let's do this thing.'"

Grayson twisted the top of the water bottle and drank heavily, his eyes fixed on his friend. After gulping down half the water, he smiled and said, "Okay, Richard. Let's do this thing."

"Gray, could you at least take me seriously for once?"

"I am taking you seriously. And I said okay."

It was Richard's turn to draw back. "Really? You're

fine with this?"

Grayson took one more drink and replaced the cap. "Yeah. Give the keys to the contractor and let's get this baby up. Why are you so surprised?"

"Because…you're never this agreeable. Normally, you're adamant about taking things on yourself and not letting others take charge. I half expected you to refuse the idea of the contractor coming in, and I planned on getting an earful of why we shouldn't open next month. So, why the change of heart?"

Grayson continued to smile. How could he not? The idea of dancing with the woman from last night, day after day, was worth smiling about. He waited for Richard to figure it out.

Richard's eyes widened. "You found a dance partner?"

Chapter Four

"Yeah. I did."

"Excellent!" Richard exclaimed, slapping his hands together. "What's her name?"

"No idea."

Richard's face fell. "You don't know her name? Then how did you meet her?"

"I met her last night at Gyrations."

"Ah, you were able to see her dance then," Richard nodded. "This is good."

"Yeah, it's good."

Richard gave him a sideways glance. "I'm assuming she left you with some type of contact information?"

Grayson turned around and put the water bottle in the fridge. "Not exactly. She left early this morning before I could ask her."

Richard's eyes widened as he drew in a deep breath. "You slept with her?"

Grayson smiled. "I did."

"Oh, don't look so proud, Gray. This is a legitimate

business we're trying to run here, not some underground escort service." Richard pinched the bridge of his nose. "And how in the hell can you bring a woman into your home, into your bed—a woman you know nothing about— and still sleep at night?" He threw up a hand, silencing Grayson. "No. Forget I asked. And wipe that smirk off your face. This isn't the least bit funny."

Grayson gave it his best shot. He smeared his grin downward with a stiff hand, but it was useless. Watching Richard sweat was truly entertaining.

"I'm serious!" his friend barked. "Don't get me wrong, I know you have impeccable taste in women, and it never ceases to amaze me the caliber of ass you've had in your possession, but sleeping with a future employee for the sake of determining her qualifications is no way to run a business. I don't need a bunch of prostitutes hanging out on the corner. I have a reputation to uphold."

"Will you relax." Grayson waved him off as he walked through his living room down the hall. "She's not a prostitute, and I've never resorted to being a john. Which, by the way, I resent." He was done with this conversation. Done with being reprimanded like an irresponsible teenager. He decided to prove his friend wrong by doing what he'd intended all along—find her and offer her the dance position.

Richard followed him into his bedroom. "How do you know she's not a prostitute? You don't even know her name, for shit's sake! For all you know, she probably skipped out with your wallet, caught a cab for New York, and is at Nordstrom's right now, buying her pimp-daddy a really nice shirt."

Without looking back at his friend, Grayson grabbed his trifold off his dresser and threw it at him.

Richard caught it. "Okay, so she's a *stupid* whore for not stealing your wallet."

"She's not a whore," Grayson corrected as he pulled out a clean pair of boxers and laid them neatly on the edge of his dresser.

Richard flipped Grayson's wallet on the bed and crossed his arms. "Fine. Let's say she's not turning tricks. What if she's just a lonely, desperate housewife and you were nothing more than a good shag on a Saturday night?"

Grayson turned his back on Richard and entered his walk-in closet where he ripped a white button-down shirt from the hanger, his irritation climbing. Richard was probably right. What if the woman's only purpose was to get laid? She kind of fit the criteria. Skipping out before sunup…never mentioning her name or asking for his. Hell, when he thought back on last night, she never even said one word.

Not a damn thing.

Grayson walked back out to face the music. His unmade bed nagged at him. Without a second's hesitation, he began making his bed while he spoke. "You and I are very different. We always have been. You were born into money. I wasn't. You found your soul mate in high school. I didn't. You've traveled the world, and I'm grounded here in Boston. But we do have one thing in common, and that is we've always trusted each other. Hence, this business arrangement. So, I'm going to ask you to find that faith in me and realize my name is on those papers too. I may not have a prestigious gallery with my name plastered across the expressways, but I have just as much invested in this club as you do. I'm not going to do anything to damage this opportunity or our friendship. But I do need you to trust me."

Richard shook his head in disbelief. "You're into this chick, aren't you?"

Grayson ran his hand through his hair, those words settling in his gut. He didn't like admitting a woman was finally able to get into his heart. But there was something different about her. Something alluring…something he had to have more of.

"Yeah, I'm into her," he admitted grudgingly. "But it's not *that* big a deal."

Richard came away from the door, peering into Grayson's eyes as if he were searching deep into his very soul. "Why? What in the hell did this woman do last night to make Grayson Anders suddenly whipped?"

He shoved his friend out of his personal space. "I don't know." He threw the shirt he was holding on top of his boxers and stormed out of the room.

Richard followed.

"I've never seen you this way before. For the first time in my life, I actually want to hear about one of your little escapades."

"Not gonna happen." Grayson saw his keys resting on the narrow table by the door—the ones his mystery woman must have picked up off the floor and kindly put there. A whore would never do that.

Oh, but a good housewife would.

A lonely, clean-freak housewife…

Not possible, he told himself. He'd seen many lonely housewives in his day and none of them were ever that quiet. Even if they were shy in the beginning, they were starving for attention and, by the end of the night, they'd be talking his ear off.

No, she wasn't a hooker, and she certainly wasn't someone's neglected wife. With a determined grip, he opened the door and waited for Richard to take the hint.

Richard stopped midway. "Joyce and I are meeting for lunch. Why don't you join us?" He smiled the way he did whenever he mentioned his wife's name. They'd been married for over fifteen years, but he still had that look in his eye as if he were newly wed.

Gray envied Richard when it came to that. Not the fact that he didn't have to work a day in his life to get where he was, or that he frequented the most exotic and lavish places in the world. Richard had been fortunate to find and marry Joyce, and that made Grayson wish he could unearth just a smidgen of that kind of good luck for himself.

Joyce was a beautiful woman, a five foot ten blonde goddess. She was just as sweet as she was sexy. What made her even more appealing was that she didn't know how damn gorgeous she was. She cared deeply about her friends and loved her family with all her heart, Richard being at the top of her list.

Lucky bastard.

"Come on, Gray… Joyce would be happy to see you. It's been a while."

Grayson smiled. "I'd love to see her too, but I've got things to do."

"Like…hiring a private investigator?"

"Cute, but no."

Richard stopped him from closing the door in his face.

"All right, fine. At least let me give you a lift to wherever you're going."

"I appreciate it, but I'm not going up town. Say hello to Joyce for me." Grayson closed the door soundly, his mind on one thing—finding the only woman who had ever left him this curious…this determined.

Chapter Five

Grayson turned the corner of his historic brownstone building in the Back Bay district of Boston—a dignified three-story complex designed by nineteenth-century architects, turned dance club—and saw his favorite cabbie, Gerry Sullivan, parked by the curb of Newbury Street.

If Big Gerry was anything, besides the obvious, he was predictable.

Every morning, Grayson would find Gerry's shiny gold taxi with its motor running, waiting to take him to his regular coffee stop at Starbucks on Beacon Street. This suited Grayson just fine. He was a man of routine, and having Gerry—a witty Irishman with a knack for being a bit off the wall—as his personal escort made the short commute anything but ordinary.

With a skip in his step, Grayson reached for the back door handle and slid inside, getting a sideways glance from Gerry as he settled into the slick, black vinyl seat.

"Late to rise today, huh? Wouldn't have anything to do with that sexy brunette skirt I took home this morning from your club, would it?"

"It might."

Gerry shook his head and looked out his side window before pulling out. "You certainly know how to pick 'em, Mr. Anders."

Grayson looked into the rearview mirror. "Why do I hear a 'but' in there?"

"Because she's not exactly your type. I mean—" Gerry stuttered. "Don't get me wrong, Mr. Anders, she's definitely not out of your league. Few women are. But she's just not the type of woman I think you'd be interested in."

Contrary to what Gerry believed, Grayson was doubly interested now. "You know her?"

"Sure. She's a painter. Artsy-fartsy kind. Owns some little shop down on Charles Street. But I think she said something about having to move—economy sucking, something like that. Course, she didn't actually say it—"

"What's her name?" Grayson interrupted.

Gerry's brows furrowed in the reflection of the rearview. "You slept with her, and you don't even know her name?"

Grayson sighed, not expecting to get judgment from a bristly cabdriver. Richard, yes. But not Big Gerry. He reached into his back pocket and pulled out his wallet, turning up a crisp hundred. He tossed it over the front seat.

"Will that help you to remember her name?"

"For that much, I can tell you what color her panties were."

"I already know that," Grayson stated with a wry grin. "I'm looking for her name, and if you take another gander, I'm betting that dead president is worth an address as well."

Gerry glanced in his rearview again with hard, serious eyes. "I could lose my job if I told you that."

"Only if your employer found out. Don't worry, I'll pay my fare separately." He let Gerry think a little as he drove east down Commonwealth, and waited until they reached the red light at Berkley before adding, "Isn't your wife's birthday coming up? You could buy her something really nice with that cash. Take her to dinner at one of those snazzy restaurants. Women love that."

Gerry merged onto Storrow. "For someone who thinks he knows so much about women, you sure have forgotten the basics, like introducing yourself."

Grayson looked out his window. No arguing there. But introductions hadn't been necessary last night. Between the two of them, there was enough chemistry to say all that was needed. They'd wanted each other from the very first glimpse into each other's eyes, and no words could have said it better than the universal language of a passionate first kiss.

Their first kiss.

Gerry cleared his throat and interrupted Grayson's pleasant daydream. "Did it ever occur to you that she didn't tell you her name 'cause she didn't want to be found?"

"It did. But I don't believe it."

With a sigh, Gerry went back to his brooding behind the wheel. As Grayson had hoped, the persuasive hundred-dollar bill sitting beside him kept the blue-collar cabbie from playing the ethical card.

"Her name is Chloe," Gerry finally muttered. "Chloe LaRoche. And I already told you she lives on Charles Street. You're not getting any more than that."

Grayson heard the irritation in Big Gerry's voice. "You're taking this a bit personally. I just asked for her name. Are you her brother or something?"

Gerry made a right at Revere and another on Charles Street before he pulled over to the curb and threw it in Park. He twisted around in his front seat and eyed Grayson intensely. "Look, Mr. Anders. Chloe isn't like any woman you've ever met."

Grayson smiled and leaned back, tossing his arm up over the seat. "I know that. I knew that the moment I laid eyes on her. That's exactly why I want to see her again."

"Then I'll put it to you straight. If you break her heart, I'm going to have to personally kick your ass."

Grayson sat up straighter in the backseat. He didn't expect to be threatened by a cabbie he'd known for years. "Whoa, big guy. I'm not going to break her heart. I just want to find her and offer her a position at Gyrations."

Gerry cocked his brow. "Chloe's not going to want to tend bar. She's an artist. She paints people in dramatic colors and positions. Stuff my wife would kill me for looking at."

"I didn't say anything about tending bar. I want a dance partner for my studio, which is opening next month, and she's the only one who's ever come close to fitting the criteria for the position."

"Are you telling me Chloe can...*dance*?"

"Yes. What's so strange about that?"

Gerry looked completely dumbfounded. "Because she's—"

"Right there!" Grayson exclaimed, pressing his face against the pane of the cab window at a brunette strolling down the sidewalk past them. "There she is! Sorry, Gerry, I have to go." He pulled a twenty from his wallet and tossed the bill in the front seat, then flung open his door as he called her name.

"Mr. Anders, wait!" Gerry yelled after him. "There's something you have to know about Chloe!"

But Grayson didn't look back. He ran down the

sidewalk, his eyes fixed on thick dark tresses and a beautiful pair of legs in black heels.

****

"Chloe!" Grayson called for the third time as he dodged between a dog-walker and an elderly man in a suit. She was definitely within earshot, but the woman never turned around. For a moment, he began to think Gerry had purposely told him the wrong name like a protective older brother would, until he finally caught up and jumped in front of her.

"Chloe," he said breathlessly, staring into a pair of dark sunglasses resting on her cute little nose. "Didn't you hear me?"

The woman slid them down and looked Grayson over thoroughly, revealing she wasn't the woman he wanted, but available nonetheless.

"Oh, I'm so sorry," Grayson apologized. "I thought you were someone else."

The woman continued to gawk at him. "She's a lucky woman."

An uncomfortable laugh escaped Grayson as he shifted his feet and shoved his hands in his pockets. He'd never been embarrassed when talking to a woman, especially one who was blatantly interested in him. So, what was so different now? "I'm sorry to bother you."

"Oh, it was no bother at all," she murmured in a deep, husky tone.

Grayson smiled politely as he walked away and looked up into the sky, knowing her eyes were glued to his butt. He wondered how many women in the past had felt the weight of *his* stare on their derrière.

Too many to count, he bet.

Trying to shake the near-salivating woman from his mind, he couldn't help but realize the change in him. By now, he would've glanced over his shoulder to check out what the woman had to offer in her trunk—without her knowing, of course—yet, he had no desire for it.

What the hell was wrong with him?

Food.

That's what he needed. It was near noon and he hadn't even had breakfast yet. He looked up from the brick-laid walk and Beacon Hill Hotel and Bistro caught his eye, with its BHHB initials on a small black sign above the door.

He loved this place. Loved the atmosphere and the stained glass behind the bar inside. He also loved the idea of scarfing down their roasted pepper frittata with onions, potatoes, and cheese. No one made a frittata quite like the Bistro.

If he had to think about it, no one knew the Beacon Hill area quite like the cute little maitre d' of the Bistro. She was a Boston native—an enthusiast, more like it—and had always helped him find the perfect meal for his dates, or saved the best table for him at a moment's notice. Perhaps she'd know where a certain artsy-fartsy painter, as Gerry called her, resided on this very street. He wasn't afraid to walk up and down this historic avenue and peer into the windows for her beautiful face if he had to.

But asking Vanessa seemed like a better idea, and less desperate.

He crossed over Chestnut Street and jaywalked to the Bistro's door, shaded by trees and a narrow green awning. He held the door for a curvy, pixie-haired blonde clutching shopping bags from nearby stores, and entered behind her, his mind only on the curves Chloe possessed.

He skirted the "bag lady," bypassed the hostess stand, and sat at the bar, barely noticing the voluptuous woman taking the order of the person beside him. He picked up a menu and flipped to the lunch section, scrolling through it out of habit, even though he already knew what he wanted. While a piping-hot, cheesy frittata sounded delicious, Chloe in his arms sounded better.

The sooner you eat, the sooner you can have her in your arms.

He cleared his throat, and the waitress looked up from

her pad. "I'll be right with you, sir."

Her coy glance gave him the impression she'd help him next, even though others were before him. She jotted a few things down on her menu pad and sauntered over to him. As her eyes drank him in, she leaned forward on the bar.

"What can I get you?"

"I'm looking for Vanessa. She working today?"

Disappointment fell across her face as she glanced around the restaurant. "She's here, but I think she's busy. Anything I can help you with?" Her eagerness was unmistakable.

"It's possible. How well do you know this area?"

"Well enough. Why?"

"I'm looking to purchase some art for my dance studio that's opening soon. I was told there's an artist who has a quaint gallery on Charles Street. Do you know where I could find it?"

"I know of one, but I'm not sure if she's got what you're looking for." Her hint was subtle, but Grayson knew exactly what she was hoping—that *she* was what he might prefer.

"Got an address?" he asked.

She sighed and tore a blank paper from her pad, then wrote it down. "She comes in here every Sunday, but I haven't seen her yet. She must have found a reason not to eat today."

"Really…" Grayson's heart leapt as he took the paper from her. "What does she order?"

"She always hands me a slip of paper with roasted turkey breast sandwich, Swiss cheese, green apples, onions, and brioche written on it. Same thing every week."

Grayson never had it, but today he'd give out of the ordinary a try. "Make that two. To go."

"Sure thing. It'll be just a few minutes."

Grayson watched as she walked out from behind the bar to place the two orders she had, her hips probably swinging just a bit more than usual. He never gave it a second thought. Instead, he glanced down at the address on the paper in his hand and smiled. He knew it was just a few blocks from here and imagined her surprise when he'd show up at her door with her favorite sandwich.

Chapter Six

Chloe couldn't believe the amount of painting she'd cranked out this afternoon. Her creation of Mr. Gyration on canvas was nearly finished. Just a few more strokes and he would be perfect. *Not that he isn't already.*

She stepped back and tilted her head, admiring her masterpiece as a whole, of her Adonis sleeping in his bed. The colors of his skin were deep brown, with just the right shading to highlight his well-toned, tanned body. The soft pastel of his cream-colored sheets, draped in a lissome array over his waist, portrayed a rare innocence about him as he lay prone. It was a distinct contrast to the hard lines of his chiseled face and muscled shoulders, which was just what she was looking for.

Chloe smiled at her achievement, her gaze washing over it one last time.

If it weren't for the wet paint, she would've reached out and touched him. Caressed his long, sinewy arm. Run her fingers through his soft black hair. Cupped his hard jaw in her palm. He was that real to her.

Oh, how her mind wouldn't let her forget about last night. Though she knew better than to think it was hardly memorable for him, she still had pleasant memories of that toe-curling, one-night stand embedded in her brain.

One-night stand.

The concept made her heart sink a little. She'd never had a one-nighter and never dreamed she ever would. But Lordy, Lordy, she had never come across a man like Mr. Gyration before either. He was every girl's fantasy and downright irresistible. Plus, it had been a long time—eons ago—since she'd been with any man.

Obviously, the odds were stacked against her. There was no way she could have walked away from him unless she was a nun, and God knew she was nowhere close to being a saint. Heck, just take one look at the front room of her gallery! There wasn't a clothed person anywhere. Every one of her paintings was a nude—a tasteful nude, she reminded herself—with no blatant frontal nudity. Leaving things to the imagination was where it was at, and, boy, was her imagination running wild over Mr. Gyration right now...for the millionth time since she awoke this morning.

Yep, no saint here.

Proud of her accomplishment, she decided to reward herself with a big juicy turkey sandwich from the Bistro. She checked her watch on her wrist. *Twelve thirty.* Right in the middle of the lunch rush, a madhouse as far as she was concerned.

Suddenly, a microwave entrée seemed more appealing. She didn't like to venture out from the safety of her home unless she had to, especially when the chances of people confronting her were higher.

She wasn't shy, but she wasn't a regular conversationalist either, especially not since her surgery back in her late college years. The doctors had removed a pair of tumors from her brain, and a part of her had been taken away with it, changing her life forever. There were things she wasn't able to do anymore and it was difficult to make such drastic alterations in her lifestyle to accommodate it. However, she did. She had no choice.

She persevered as best she could, but she'd give anything to reverse time and live out her days like she used to, without the lengthy stares or whispers from those who realized she was different.

Her parents encouraged her never to think of her situation as a handicap. But it was.

She couldn't mingle with just anyone at parties. She couldn't get into a conversation with most strangers at a bus stop. She couldn't even order her food like a normal person at a restaurant. Her days of having a normal life were over. If she had been born with it, she'd probably feel differently. She'd probably not even notice what she was missing, and she could look at herself with pride.

But having had something all your life and then losing it in the blink of an eye was incredibly difficult to overcome and harder to endure as time went on.

The only thing she could still do that she loved was dance. Well, as long as the music was loud enough and the bass was helping her to keep time with the rhythm.

Dance.

It was what she'd wanted to do from the time she was little, have a career dancing on stage, performing for people, entertaining them, and expressing her creative side with movement and grace.

That ship had sailed.

The only way for her to express herself now was through her art.

Sure, people said her talent with the brush far outweighed her ability with choreographed movement. She could now see why, especially since her paintings had gained several prestigious, though small, awards. But it was still hard to say good-bye to her dancing ambitions.

She glanced at her canvas, gazing at the man who hadn't noticed her shortcoming last night. She smiled. He was the only person who hadn't looked down on her or deemed her incapable. In fact, he never even seemed to notice. He'd encouraged her to dance, to express herself freely without fearing what others might think, and to believe in herself again.

She remembered feeling a bit envious of his confidence when he'd first taken her hand and led her to the dance floor. But the moment he swept her into his arms and told her to hold on tight, she forgot all about her self-consciousness, and the crowd around her. She cared only for the man who stared into her eyes. The one man who looked at her as if he'd finally found his perfect dance mate. The only partner for him.

No one had ever looked at her like that. No one had ever seen beyond the surface and into the woman within.

Her heart swelled as she remembered the other things he'd seen. Unlike her tasteful paintings with just enough left to the imagination, there was no part of her unexplored, untouched. He had stripped her bare of both her clothing and her inhibitions. There was nothing left to hide.

In all honesty, when she looked back on last night, she should have felt cheap and easy. When she woke up this morning, she should have felt dirty and full of regret. But she didn't. There wasn't an ounce of regret on her conscience—not one iota.

If anything, her spirits had lifted as if she had wings to fly.

Hugging her paintbrush to her chest, she twirled around on her heels and let out a scream of sheer happiness. She ran to the coffee table in her open studio apartment, snatched the remote, and turned on the TV, which was always set to Sirius XM—the Latin channel.

"Tonight (I'm Loving You)" by Enrique Iglesias was already playing.

One of her favorites.

She pressed the volume button until the hard bass boomed from her surround-sound speakers, and danced to her heart's content. She closed her eyes and gyrated around the floor, holding her brush to her chest as if Mr. Gyration were pressed against her. She had no trouble imagining him leading her around the dance floor, his pelvis moving against hers, his hands fanning across her lower back, his soulful tawny eyes holding her captive…

****

CLOSED.

Grayson read the sign in the window, and his heart sank. He checked the address again on the paper the waitress had given him and confirmed the number above the door. Stuffing the paper back in his pocket, he sighed, wondering what to do with his double order of sandwiches.

He wanted to surprise Chloe, but it appeared she wasn't available.

…till he heard music.

Loud music, coming from inside.

He put his ear closer to the door and listened.

She had Enrique Iglesias playing—no, blaring.

He chuckled as he came away from the door, looking around to see if anyone else passing by heard the booming cadence coming from within her gallery. Apparently, a few people. He even saw one guy step up his walk to the beat, shaking his hips to the rhythm, and earning an elbow from his unimpressed girlfriend.

Grayson cupped his hand above his brow and peered into the window. He couldn't see her inside, but at least he knew she was home…or working…or dancing. Whatever she was doing, she didn't seem to want to be disturbed. The Closed sign hanging against the pane and the music so loud she was risking breaking several ordinances were two big indications.

But Grayson had never been known for his reservation.

He tried knocking, and the door moved. Surprised to see it unlocked, he pushed it open.

He glanced around first and then entered, his excitement building. It was quite unusual for him to care this much about seeing one specific woman, about being with her. He enjoyed the newness and rolled with it.

Inside, numerous paintings hung on the walls. Each one was better than the last.

He took in the colors, the twisting of half-naked bodies, and their sensual positions. To him, each couple looked as if they were entangled in a dance. If a psychologist were to hold each of these canvases up as an ink-blot test, he'd respond the same on each one. He might mix it up a bit and say that particular one was the tango. This one was the rumba. And that one, on the far corner, was the paso doble.

One thing was for sure, Chloe LaRoche had talent.

She could take a fleshy, near-pornographic image and turn it into a beautiful display of sumptuous, erotic art. Just what his dance studio needed.

At the change of a song, his attention moved from the paintings and into the gallery as a whole. It smelled like paint and wood and Chloe. He could distinctly remember the scent of her skin from last night, and it lingered all around him now. Oh, how he loved the way she smelled. Clean, with a hint of vanilla.

He walked around the small gallery, finding himself idly shopping for artwork to hang on his soon-to-be-a-studio walls. But this one, he decided as he drew closer to the register desk, was different. Hanging at eye level behind the cash register, it portrayed a solitary female with polished ivory skin and long dark hair draped over one shoulder. He doubted Chloe had painted such a revealing self-portrait, especially with so much detail and…skin. But he swore it looked exactly like her. From the soft arch of her hips to the modest swell of her breasts covered by her slender arm laid across her chest.

He drew even closer, leaning across the counter.

Yeah, that was her, all right.

He pictured it hanging in his bedroom, and envisioned the dark-auburn hues of her painted hair coordinating well with the deep woodgrain of his cherry furniture.

Yes, that one he'd buy for himself.

As he continued to stretch across the counter, a paper blew onto the floor. When he picked it up, the bright red wording at the top, which read: 2nd NOTICE, caught his eye. He glanced over the receipt. It seemed Chloe was behind on her lease and had been given her final warning from the landlord. He swallowed, knowing this was not his business to be reading her personal mail, and quickly returned the paper to the counter.

Poor Chloe. He didn't like knowing she struggled to make ends meet, especially someone with her talent. Someone like her should be selling paintings left and right, with no worries of when the next paycheck would fall.

He shouldn't care so much; he barely knew her. But for some reason, he felt protective of her and wanted to help her through her financial difficulties. He'd never given thought to sharing his wealth with a woman before. In fact, he steered clear of women who were gold diggers and leeches.

Chloe was different.

She hadn't pursued him at the club like most women had. She hadn't even stuck around the apartment the next morning for him to buy her breakfast. She was mysterious. Unpredictable. And, until he'd walked into her shop, elusive.

Perhaps those things were what drew her to him so strongly. A challenge. The thrill of the hunt...

He glanced toward a door to the side of the counter, from where the loud music was coming—where Chloe no doubt was. A strange sense of possessiveness came over him. To see her. To capture her. To claim her.

Was he out of his freakin' mind?

She was a woman with baggage—the heaviest of all kinds, money problems. If he walked through that door, he might be in for a hell of a lot more than what he bargained for. And since he'd already slept with her, it would be nigh on impossible for him to back out.

Save face, Grayson, and walk out the door.

But he couldn't.

He wanted to see her again, to see her look of surprise. To have her in his arms again.

Last night was the most incredible night he had ever had, and he wanted more of those nights. With her.

Who gives a crap if she's a struggling artist? Every person with a dream struggles at one point or another. Even him, years ago.

And let's not forget the reason you pursued her in the first place. If she takes your offer of employment at Gyrations, the extra cash would surely help her.

Grayson liked the sound of that. It lightened the burden of assisting her without the notion of her picking from his pockets. No one else could allege such a thing later on either. There was nothing he wanted more than to dance with this woman day after day and, quite possibly, score himself a sexy, provocative lover to boot.

The unrelenting female club hounds of Gyrations will be thoroughly pissed.

He smiled, pleased that his dueling opinions came to some agreement. Her baggage be damned, Grayson Anders was going to pay his little enigmatic vixen a visit.

The moment he opened the door, his bravado left him. She was dancing around her quaint efficiency apartment in nothing but baggy dove-gray sweats and a paint-splotched

T-shirt. She was the sexiest woman he'd ever seen.

Yep, he was a goner.

Her cute little bottom bumped and grinded to David Bisbal's "Oye El Boom," her legs slightly bent, her eyes closed. She held a paintbrush in one hand, pressing it close to her chest, while her other hand smoothed down her hip.

She hadn't noticed him standing there, but he sure noticed the twitch in his groin as he ached to be her paintbrush. Watching Chloe was like watching his own personal erotic dancer—whetting all his senses with tantalizing shoulder rolls and hip thrusts—minus the pole and the cover charge to view her.

This whole situation was perfect. He was able to catch a glimpse of Chloe LaRoche behind closed doors and see that she enjoyed dancing just as much as he did—and to the same style of music he listened to. Too many women in his life had pretended to like Latin-style dancing simply to win his affection. But as he stood in his remote corner of the room, the real Chloe unfolded right before his eyes. He was truly smitten.

Unable to be the inactive spectator any longer, he set their Styrofoam to-go lunches on the floor and walked toward her. With the music blaring in her ears, his hunger to touch her drove him to dance with her. He slipped his hands around her waist and pulled her into his arms.

"Mind if I join you?"

****

Chloe gasped, her heart frozen in her chest. Just as quickly as she feared for her life, she melted at the sight of her Adonis's beautiful face smiling at her. Was he real?

Oh yes, he was real.

His strong hands flattened across her lower back, bordering on her butt, and pulled her tighter in his embrace. His eyes delved deep into hers.

How did he find her? And how the hell did he get in here?

I swore the door was locked and the Closed sign was up.

She stiffened, despite the fluid motion of his hips swaying to the beat of the music. She lost all sense of rhythm and awkwardly followed his lead, wondering if she'd made a huge mistake sleeping with this guy in the first place. Maybe he was crazy out of his mind? Maybe he was an ax murderer on the side.

He drew back, softening his embrace. "I didn't mean to frighten you. You left your outside door unlocked. But don't worry, I secured it behind me. Besides," he added, spinning her, "your music was up so loud, I doubt you would've heard me knock anyway."

Chloe smiled nervously, her mind going a thousand miles an hour.

She talked herself out of thinking he was an ax murderer, but he could very well be a trained burglar. She couldn't believe he'd snuck into her shop and made his way into her meager apartment. She glanced around, checking the condition of it, worrying about what he'd think of her modest living conditions. They were quite different from his.

His home looked like something out of *Architectural Digest*, a penthouse suite of some famous actor in downtown New York. While hers resembled a barely middle-class, single-income dive, with drop cloths on the floor and artist supplies resting on every flat surface.

He stopped dancing, his forehead scrunching. "Can you turn this down? I can barely hear myself think."

Chloe swallowed hard and nodded, leaving him in haste to find the remote on the table. She aimed it at the TV and pressed the volume button, her heartbeat climbing as the volume fell.

She stared at it, lost. It was inevitable he would find out about her secret, but she wasn't prepared to tell him now. Truthfully, she'd never imagined there'd be an opportunity to explain or a need to. She'd left his bed this morning thinking she would never see him again. But her perfect Adonis had surprisingly thought enough about her to go searching, and since he succeeded, his adamancy spoke volumes.

She detected his presence behind her and turned around, his arms already crisscrossing her back.

"Just because the music is turned low doesn't mean I'm finished dancing."

He began gyrating his hips against hers and fanned his hands across her bottom. She followed his lead, though she still couldn't believe he was here. In her home. Looking at her again with that same insatiable lust she became accustomed to in his eyes.

And why? She wasn't dressed in tight-fitting clothes or even an outfit that revealed a large amount of skin or cleavage. She was wearing sweats, for crying out loud!

As if reading her conflicted mind, he nudged his nose with hers. "You are so beautiful, you know that?"

His words flattered her immensely, but she could tell by the look in his eyes that he actually meant them. She closed hers, taking pleasure in his skillful hands moving up her sides, his palms skimming over every single rib as he went. His thumbs lingered just beneath her breasts.

Okay, so he wasn't a trained burglar. But he was an extremely talented and generous lover. Her stomach flipped, and she glanced at his mouth, wanting to taste his lips. To give him whatever he'd come for. She knew right then he wasn't going to take it unless she offered it. He may have been boldly intrusive when he snuck into her residence, but now he didn't seem so self-assured. Could it be that her arrogant Adonis wasn't so haughty after all? Or maybe…a gentleman?

She wasn't the cruel type to make him sweat it out. She ran her hands up the length of his arms, enjoying the hard flex of his biceps beneath her palms as she continued over his shoulders and up his neck into his hair. Pulling him down slightly, she stood on tiptoes and kissed him.

The softness of his lips melted her like butter, while the prickling of his goatee turned her into a covetous woman. She had to have more. His mouth. His touch. His body. Everything he possessed, she wanted. She took his passion and ran free with it. Her tongue slipped between his lips, soft and warm.

"Is this just like last night?" he asked, panting against her lips. "Sex now…talk later?"

She nodded and ripped her T-shirt over her head with more exuberance than she cared to admit. He worked over every button like a wild man trying to catch up. After he whisked away his shirt, he tugged her back into his arms again.

She sighed at the comfort of his strong, warm embrace

enveloping her. She glanced over his shoulder at her newly painted canvas. It was as if her sleeping Adonis had awakened, stepped right off the easel, and come to thank her for bringing life to him.

If only he knew how alive she felt to be in his arms...

He pulled her down to the floor and lay on top of her. A large block-pattered area rug acted as their bed. She didn't care where he chose to take her. Anywhere with him bordered on heavenly.

She pushed him to the side and rolled on top, straddling him. His eyes widened, and he arched in pain. "Wait!" He reached beneath him and pulled out a tube of paint, most of it squeezed out on his hand and back.

Chloe brought a hand to her mouth and hid her smile. She hadn't realized it had dropped on the floor, but in this little apartment, there wasn't much room for storing her tools and supplies.

As he tried to wipe the mess from his back, the soft yellow color smeared across his dark skin, and the thick, oily paint covered his hand. Compelled to be daring, she grabbed his hand, hooked a dollop on her finger, and began drawing the letter "M" right above his navel.

His head jerked and his abdomen flexed beneath her. But she continued to write.

"I."

Then an "N."

And then finally an "E."

She watched his expression turn devious. "Oh, really..." he said, relaxing back onto the carpet. "Prove it."

Chloe raised her brows, reveling in his dare. Little did he know, her entire adult life had been led in defiance of a dare, proving people wrong. Especially after her surgery, she constantly had to prove she could live a normal life and succeed at it. Her small business attested to that.

Accepting his challenge, she wiped the residual paint across her own stomach in a suggestive manner and undid the button on his fly. The word "MINE" held her attention.

Yes...for a little while, he was hers—all hers. But she couldn't help but wonder how long he'd stick around.

Chapter Seven

On the floor, he lay sprawled upon her, sweat clinging to their spent bodies. Chloe aimlessly stroked her nails up and down his back, relishing every breath he took. She could hold him all day long. She didn't even need to eat.

Her stomach argued differently.

Mr. Gyration lifted his head from her chest. "Sounds like you're hungry. Well, you're in luck. I brought food."

He slipped from her embrace and padded barefoot across her floor, his beautifully toned backside bringing a smile to her face. Chloe sat up, enjoying the view. He seemed very comfortable with his nakedness, as if they'd known each other longer than twenty-four hours. She felt the complete opposite. There was no way to hide her secret any longer.

Her stomach knotted, and her mouth went dry.

Even as he bent to pick up two Styrofoam containers from the floor, a sight that should have been so pleasing to her eyes, her guilt distracted her. Not for what she was about to tell him, but because she hadn't told him yet.

She would have told him early this afternoon had he not looked at her with those stunningly mesmeric eyes. Touched her with those hot, masculine hands.

There hadn't been a decent opportunity to tell him.

She looked around for a shirt, something to hide her nakedness for when she opened her soul to him. Everything was too far out of reach. She bit her lip as he came back to their spot on the floor and sat beside her.

"I brought a surprise for you. Hope I got it right."

Chloe glanced at the lunch he presented and forced a smile. Suddenly, she didn't feel all that hungry. Sick was more like it.

Just tell him!

She caught him staring at her as if she'd never eaten take-out before, and he'd just revealed a modern miracle.

"Come on, say something," he encouraged. "I brought your favorite sandwich from Beacon Hill Bistro, and all I get is a half smile?" He set the food down next to him and reached out, cupping her chin in his large hand. "Give me something, beautiful. I've never heard your voice, and I'm betting it purrs like a kitten."

Chloe closed her eyes and pushed his hand away. This was it. The moment she'd been dreading since the first time he brushed against her arm at the bar. The moment that would determine what kind of man her Adonis was. She didn't think he'd be so shallow as to judge her by her faults, but she couldn't be sure. She didn't know him well enough.

"What's wrong?" he asked, scooting closer. "Cat got your tongue?"

She sat up straighter and took a deep breath. She brought her hands in front of her, paused, and signed the words, *"I'm deaf."*

Chloe watched him draw back in surprise and then his brows lowered in confusion. "What are you doing? What does that mean?"

A heavy breath escaped her, and sheer dread pushed her down to rock bottom. She stood to find a piece of paper and a pen from her tiny kitchenette, shaking as she tried to write. She tore the slip and handed him the sticky note.

He stood in front of her, warily taking it from her hands. He glanced down at the simple sentence.

I'm deaf.

His gaze shot back at her. "Are you serious?"

She nodded reluctantly.

"But…you danced with me," he argued. "Like no one I'd ever seen. You danced with me at Gyrations and…today." His justifications fell like autumn leaves in the wind, each one a futile attempt to oppose her profound hearing loss. "You danced…keeping perfect time with the rhythm. How can you do that if you can't hear?"

She started to sign again, but he rudely waved her off.

"I can't understand what you're doing. Write it down."

Hot tears burned her cheeks as she wrote her reply.

This time, he snatched the paper from her, irritation written across his ignorant face.

I used to dance. But I lost my hearing eight years ago. I know what rhythm is, and I can still keep time if the music is loud enough for me to feel it.

He looked at her again, but his eyes weren't a warm amber anymore. They were cold, dark, and narrow. She swallowed hard, waiting. She gripped the pen tightly, fearing he was about to turn from her and run.

He stepped forward, nearly into her, touching her elbows with both hands. "You can't be deaf. I talked to you, and you understood every word I said."

Good. This was good. He was touching her, staying close, wanting to be close to her. He was still denying her hearing loss, which was normal. It was the first stage of any sort of bereavement. She had to yield to it, let him wander through this phase so he'd be able to freely move on to the next.

But she knew what the next one was—anger. And she didn't know if she was strong enough to withstand it.

Despite the warmth of his touch on her arms, she

trembled inside. She tried to steady her hand as she wrote her next note. *I can read your lips. Not many can, but I have a knack for it.*

He tossed the paper aside and rubbed his hand over his clenched jaw. He stepped back and pondered. After a few agonizing seconds, he bent and grabbed his clothes from the floor.

"I can't believe this," he muttered, shoving his legs into his pants.

Chloe endured his hard glare as he buttoned his jeans and threw on his shirt. Her heart ached as she watched him get ready to walk out of her life. A painful lump hardened in her throat.

"Why didn't you tell me?" he demanded, staring at her as if he'd been stabbed in the back.

Automatically, and as quickly as she could, she signed the words, *"I wanted to. But—"*

He threw his palm up, closing his eyes. "Don't. I can't understand it anyway. Let's just forget we ever met, because clearly this…this would never work between us. And to think I came here because I wanted you to be my dance partner for my studio that's opening at the end of next month." He scoffed at the sound of it. "I don't know what the hell I was thinking."

He looked at her one last time. Was that remorse in his

eyes? Was he about to recant all he'd said and hold on to what he'd felt for her? She knew he didn't love her, but she was certainly hoping he'd remember just how enthralled he'd been by her. So much so that he'd gone out of his way to find out who she was, where she lived, and what sandwich she liked to eat on Sundays.

Hope.

Chloe hung on to that tiny thread with all she had.

But he looked away, his hands on his hips, and shook his head. She didn't have to see his expression to know he was chastising himself for being foolish enough to fall for her.

Without another glance, he put on his shoes and left.

Chapter Eight

Grayson stepped out of Chloe's gallery, still in shock.

I'm deaf.

Those words ran him over like a steamroller, over and over. How could he not know this? How could he be so stupid not to pick up on something as obvious as a woman who couldn't hear a lick?

Was he that blind? Was he that stupid not to see the signs?

He replayed last night over in his head, from the moment he'd walked up to the bar, to the moment he dragged her out on the dance floor. She never made a peep. Then again, he never said anything to warrant a reply either. They'd remained locked in each other's arms, captured by each other's eyes, unable to separate. Words hadn't been necessary.

All he remembered was wanting her, aching to be close to her. Nothing else, not even her name, seemed important at the time.

If only he'd struck up a conversation like a normal

person last night, instead of coming on to her like a deer in rut, he would have realized the huge language barrier between them. Or, at least put his brakes on, for shit's sake. More importantly, he wouldn't be standing here now, looking like a dumb ass.

He shook his head, disappointed. He was so excited to have finally found a woman who danced as well as he, and loved to do so. He saw it with his own eyes.

But how? How could a woman who couldn't hear, be better than all the others who could? It didn't make any sense. What puzzled him more was how Chloe had affected him. Even now, he couldn't shake her from his mind. He liked the "gotta find her" compulsion he'd woken up with this morning and the strange, never-before longing that consumed him in his search. Even if he did enjoy what she'd brought, it would never work out between them. He had no idea how to sign his words, and he sure as hell couldn't foresee learning.

He reflected on all the things he'd miss out on with her. Normal conversations over candlelit dinners. Those cute little inside jokes between lovers. The sound of her voice whispering in his ear. There'd be none of that.

And there'd be no nights spent dancing to soft, romantic music either.

He loved the thought of doing that with a woman—

with her—but she'd have to have it so loud, the neighbors would be calling the cops every night for disturbing the peace.

Shoving his hands in his pockets, he pushed away all thoughts of Chloe LaRoche and tried to figure out the bigger picture: who was he going to partner with for the opening of his studio next month?

With less than six weeks to find someone, he was screwed. He tossed around the idea of the blonde chick who frequented Gyrations nearly every weekend. She was the next best choice. Unfortunately, she came with drama and she was far too young for his taste.

Dammit.

Chloe was his *only best* choice. His perfect choice in every way, except for…

He grumbled another inward curse, staring at each uneven red brick passing beneath his feet. The farther he got from her gallery, the more he wanted to turn back around and apologize.

What an ass. Even if he did go back, she wouldn't accept his apology. He didn't deserve forgiveness anyway, not after what he said to her and how he treated her on the way out. He'd given her the cold shoulder, even when hot tears welled in her eyes.

He'd hurt her. He'd hurt her bad. And Chloe was not a

pushover. She clearly wasn't the kind of woman who relied on others, and she sure as hell didn't need him. That was apparent the moment he'd woken up and found her gone from his bed.

So, why did he need *her?*

He'd never needed anyone. Never. But Chloe had somehow slipped her pretty little self into his heart and set up camp. Sure, he was desperate for a dance partner, but it went far deeper than that. He needed her in his life. He needed her within reach to touch her, to smell the warm vanilla scent of her hair as he breathed her in.

Yeah, he was still a goner. A sucker for her beauty, her talents, and her kiss…

He had to forget about it.

Had to forget about her.

It would never work, he reminded himself

Grayson walked aimlessly for what seemed like hours, making his way through historic Boston, his mind replaying things over and over: their first dance at Gyrations, their first kiss in the stairwell, their first night together…which happened to be the best night of his life.

He also rummaged through his actions this afternoon… When he had watched her dance. When he had joined her. And, of course, when he had hot, delicious sex with her. Again.

She was the most beautiful thing he'd ever seen, and Lord knew he had seen his share of gorgeous women. It came with the territory of being a dancer and the owner of a successful, happening club. Chloe was more than just a pretty face. She was independent, a big plus on his scale of first-rate qualities, and if he was tallying traits, he could add intriguing and extremely artistically gifted to the list.

But how could he be with a woman who couldn't hear? How could he be with a woman who couldn't hear music, the most important thing in his very being, his core, his soul? Music was the very thing that made him who he was. He lived and breathed for music, for dancing.

It didn't seem possible, the two of them. They were opposite poles that defied the laws of physics. They would never attract.

"How'd it go this afternoon, Mr. Anders?"

Grayson looked up from his view of the sidewalk and saw Big Gerry sitting curbside in his taxi, his head out the window. Grayson sighed and looked at his watch. "Aren't you supposed to be off the clock by now?"

Gerry got out of the car. "I'm not offering to give you a lift. I'm asking how your day with Chloe went."

"How do you think it went?" Grayson snarled.

"Well, judging by the look on your face...not too well. I'm just hoping you're a bigger man than what I have you pegged for right now."

"Come on, Gerry. I'm not in the mood."

Gerry neared him, backing him against the wall of his building. "You're not in the mood? Fine. Let's talk of something else. Like what kind of mood Chloe's in right now."

Grayson stared the cabbie down, knowing he'd better answer carefully, given Big Gerry's threat this morning. But his hesitation was an even bigger mistake. "You sonofabitch" was the last thing Grayson heard before he took a solid fist in the mouth that knocked him into next Sunday.

Staggering against the wall, he cradled his jaw. "What the—"

Gerry grabbed him by his shirt and straightened him against the building. "You want another? Or are you going to step into my office"—he gestured toward the cab behind him—"so we can discuss this in private?"

"Hey, buddy." A voice resounded out over the ringing in Grayson's ears. "You want me to call the cops?"

Grayson looked past Big Gerry's wide shoulders at a witness with a cell phone in hand, then back at Gerry, who didn't look the least bit threatened. If anything, Gerry looked as if he was daring Grayson to say yes.

"Nah," Grayson muttered. "It's cool. I deserved it."

"Damn right you did," Gerry huffed, releasing him.

There was a hint of remorse in Gerry's eyes, but Grayson didn't push it. He simply touched his sore lip and glanced at his bloodstained fingertips. "You want a job as a bouncer?"

Gerry scoffed, and a smile cracked his hardened face. "Hardly. Now, are we gonna talk in private, or you want to finish it out here where we've got an audience?"

Grayson pushed off the wall, noticing the small gathering of bystanders around them. He wasn't in the mood to talk this out with anyone, but he knew he wasn't going to get anywhere without first coming clean with Gerry.

He waved off the lingering spectators and made haste for the door of the cab. Both men got in from the driver's side and stared at each other, Gerry in the front seat and Grayson in the back.

"I'm going to assume by the might of your punch you are, indeed, Chloe's protective older brother," Grayson stated, tenderly touching his swollen lip again.

"Protective? Yes. Brother? No. So, what happened with her?"

"Why do you care so much?"

"Let's just say I don't like people who take advantage of others."

"Considering I had no idea Chloe was deaf, how could I have taken advantage of her? Besides, she doesn't seem like the type who'd allow it anyway."

"Are you gonna tell me what happened? Or do I have to ask her?"

Grayson dropped his head back on the leather seat. "Look, she told me she was deaf. I was floored. I didn't know what to say. I stumbled around on my words…and I just left."

Gerry shook his head. "With all due respect, Mr. Anders, you are an asshole."

Grayson could hardly argue with the man. "Thanks for pointing that out for me. Are we done here?"

Gerry ignored him and wrote something down. "Do you like her?"

"What are you, my shrink?"

Gerry looked at him askance. "I'm going to take that, and the fact that you walked all the way home with guilt and sadness, as a yes. So, here," he said, handing him a simple phone number on a business-card-size note. "Call her."

Grayson took the paper, looking at the digits as if they were a useless string of lottery numbers. "Hello? She's deaf…"

"She's deaf, Mr. Anders. But she's not a mute to

society." He rubbed his temples. "She runs her own business, for God's sake." The cabbie paused, allowing Grayson a minute to catch up. "When you call the number, you'll be speaking to an interpreter. It's a service—VRS. Google it. Someone will interpret your message for Chloe—live—and Chloe's response will be spoken back to you. Call her."

Amazement settled around Grayson. He had no idea a service like this even existed. As big of a revelation as that was, he sure as hell couldn't believe he was still drawn to her. Just like when he'd accidentally seen her late lease notice. For some reason, he'd been concerned for her then, and he was still concerned for her now.

What was he doing going soft for a woman like this? He was just asking for a world of drama—a noose he swore he'd never willingly put his neck in.

He looked at Gerry now, hoping to get by on an excuse. "Even if I did call her…I wouldn't know what to say. I wouldn't know where to begin."

"Flip it over," Gerry suggested. "You can start there."

He read the name and the title. "Brigit Sullivan: Interpreter for the Deaf and Hearing Impaired."

"That's my sister. She's how I met Chloe and why I'm her personal cabbie whenever she needs a lift somewhere. Kind of like you."

Grayson took a deep breath, flipping the card between his fingertips. He had so many mixed emotions right now, about Chloe, about him and Chloe together, about everything. And sitting in the backseat of a cab with Big Gerry hovering wasn't helping him. He tucked the card into his breast pocket and stared out the window, looking at nothing.

"She wasn't always deaf, you know," Gerry added. "She used to be a dancer. A good one, from what I understand. Ballet, or something like that. Had a promising career."

Grayson's heart melted. A dancer... It all made sense now. "How'd she lose her hearing?"

"Some sort of brain tumors when she was in college. Bilateral something neuroma. I dunno. Brigit knows the term. Ask her. Chloe tried to keep dancing, but after the surgery, she lost her equilibrium and her hearing. The balance comes back, I'm told, but the permanent hearing loss comes with the removal of the tumors. Most times, the hearing loss isn't so severe. But in Chloe's case, the tumors were so large, the doctors had to cut into her skull from behind her ear to remove them."

Grayson felt about as low as a man could feel. How could he be so insensitive? He tried to put himself in her place but couldn't imagine having to give up dancing. It must have been excruciatingly difficult for her to accept and doubly hard to pick herself up from rock bottom and carry on. He thought of her paintings, her new life as an artist—a remarkably talented artist—and the struggles she was having establishing herself.

He cursed himself, recalling the way he'd treated her. The way he'd left her standing there, tears in her eyes as if she couldn't possibly say anything worth his time.

God, he was an ass. An egotistical bastard.

"I have a lot to think about."

"Well, while you're pondering, perhaps you could squeeze in a little compassion for Chloe. You know, think of someone else besides yourself for a change... If you're even capable."

Grayson exited the cab and put his hand on the roof as he leaned toward the driver's-side window. "Thanks," he said, rubbing his jaw.

"Don't mention it. It was my pleasure, Mr. Anders."

"I'm sure it was." Grayson tapped the roof twice. "See you tomorrow morning."

Chapter Nine

Chloe stared at the label on the flattened Winsor & Newton tube of paint as if it held an emotional significance. For any other painter, Naples Yellow Light No. 426 was just another dull shade on the color spectrum. For her, it would always remind her of what she'd had and lost.

MINE. She'd spelled it out on the plane of his stomach, and, for a few blessed moments in her life, she thought he actually welcomed the idea. *Surely he did, else he wouldn't have dared me to prove it.* But somewhere between his playful challenge and his abrupt withdrawal, she'd let him slip through her fingers. By the look in his eyes, she knew she'd never see her Adonis again.

Choking back the urge to cry, she tossed the empty tube of paint in the trash on top of the carryout order from The Bistro. She'd lost her appetite, unable to stomach one bite of the turkey sandwich. The only thing that hadn't vanished were musings of how he'd found her so quickly and how he'd come to know her regular Sunday meal. How could a man who was so meticulous in his investigation be so shallow?

As if it mattered now…

Tying up the garbage bag, she said farewell to the meal and the nostalgic pastel hue she'd used on both him and the canvas. Never again would she look at that color the same, nor could she keep looking at her "Adonis at Rest" sitting on the easel. Though she'd painted it for the sole purpose of holding on to a blissful memory, she couldn't bear the pain that was now associated with it. Like the empty tube of paint, it also had to go.

Her gaze drifted longingly toward the canvas. Its subject, though quite passive in nature, taunted her. She'd never painted anything as beautiful as her sleeping divinity, and she'd never produced a work of still life art in a matter of hours. Being a perfectionist, she'd normally paint for days, if not weeks, altering brushstrokes, smoothing gradations, and fussing over shadows. This piece came out of nowhere, in the same way Mr. Gyration had come into her life. Unfortunately, he left just as swiftly, leaving behind tears and open wounds.

She turned her back on the artistic composition silently tormenting her from the corner of the room and trudged toward the shower. While a small part of her was angry for the way he'd walked out on her, a larger portion pitied herself for not being able to hold on to him.

She knew she shouldn't beat herself up, for he didn't deserve to be the focus of her emotional strain. She had enough to worry about as it was, and there were plenty of other men worth painting. Hell, if one couldn't be readily found, her wild and creative imagination could just as easily conjure up the next best thing. But when it came to finding a man who finally made her feel alive and special, at this dismal moment, no one compared.

This was why she didn't do casual sex. It was why she didn't do casual anything. Casual often included a streak of recklessness, which usually led to shame and regret, and the last thing she had ever wanted to do was regret meeting Mr. Gyration.

Too late for that now.

****

Grayson unlocked the door to his third-story apartment and entered his home, the combined noise of pounding hammers and whirling sanders resonating through the floor below. Drawing the chain lock, he'd never been so thankful to be away from everyone. Away from the crowded streets of Boston. Away from his nosy cabbie. Away from the adamant contractor who spotted him sneaking up the stairwell and insisted on getting his signature on an approval and a waiver. Everyone.

So why couldn't he get away from Chloe?

All he could think about was her beautiful face, the way she smiled at him whenever he'd taken her in his arms and danced with her. He realized now she was probably thrilled to have been able to dance again. To have shared that dance with a man who wanted it just as much. Yet he'd brutally cast her dreams aside. He'd shattered her very soul by calling attention to her impairment and coldly shoving it in her face.

He threw his keys on the table and walked to his bedroom, stopping short when he saw his reflection in the mirror hanging above his dresser. He stared back at a shallow, self-centered man and hated what he saw. Many times he'd looked in that mirror and seen a man who had so much to offer: money and success; a handsome face on a graceful, athletically built body, all rolled into one total package. A decent catch as far as most women were concerned.

But now…he saw an empty shell, nothing more than a man who was as vacant as a cheap, drive-by trucker motel. He wasn't worth a second look, and he sure as hell wasn't worth Chloe's tears, not after what he'd done to her.

As he methodically unbuttoned his shirt, ready to get comfortable and veg out, he caught a glimpse of something yellow. Like a brand, he saw the smeared paint of the word "MINE" written across his stomach above his denim waistband.

He'd forgotten all about her playful antics with the paint, the way she seductively painted herself before...

His knees almost gave out. As vividly as if she were there in front of him, he could feel the warmth of her body and the look of sheer happiness in her beautiful dark eyes.

He staggered to his bed and sat down. She'd claimed him. But it seemed she'd seized more of him than what the conspicuous letters painted on him declared.

How could this be? How had Chloe LaRoche been able to slip past his guard and capture his heart without him even knowing?

He fell back against the mattress and stared at the ceiling. The bigger question was why did he have to make such a big deal of her hearing loss and use it as an excuse not to be with her. Clearly, his ignorance was the only thing keeping them apart. Shock played a major factor, he supposed. Maybe even a little shame for not noticing her deafness on his own. But no matter how much he tried to deny it, he was just a conceited, pathetic schmuck who'd perceived her lack of hearing as a handicap, and God forbid his perfect dance partner have a flaw.

He groaned, hating how shallow and insensitive that

sounded. He was deeply sorry for every bit of it; so much that he wanted to make it up to her. Apologize. He'd drop to his knees if he had to.

Would she even accept it?

Since she was deaf, he knew she could easily turn her back on him, refusing to read his lips, and never know a word he said.

No, an apology wouldn't be enough. He'd stepped on her heart and trampled all over her pride. It would take more than a few contrite words to amend those things. Whatever he did, it had to be big. It had to be momentous enough that she'd think twice about slamming the door in his face.

He reached into his breast pocket and pulled out the business card, staring at the ten numbers scratched on the back. Oh, how he wanted to call her.

But no. It was too soon.

First things first.

He retrieved his cell from his jeans and stabbed two buttons. He closed his eyes and put the phone to his ear, waiting for his friend to pick up.

"Hey, Gray!" Richard's voice broke through. "What's up?"

Grayson sat still for a moment, not sure what to say.

"Gray? You there?"

"Yeah, I'm here." Grayson sat up. "Am I interrupting anything?"

"No, not at all. I'm just driving back to the office."

Grayson remembered Richard's lunch date with his wife and checked the time on the alarm clock next to his bed. "You're just now heading back from lunch with Joyce?"

A typical I-got-laid-on-my-lunch-hour laugh came through. "What's it to you?"

"And you left your wife to go back to the office? It's Sunday."

"Yeah, well…duty calls, my friend."

That was Richard. Always working.

"So, what's up? You're fishing. Spit it out."

Grayson gave a tight laugh and scratched his head. "I have a favor to ask."

"Oh shit. What now?"

"Just hear me out. It might benefit you."

"I'm listening," Richard said skeptically.

"I was down on Charles Street today, looking for some things for the studio…"

"Yeah."

"And I found an artist who might be right up your alley for the big exhibition you got coming up."

"Gray," Richard interrupted, "I'm not looking to

showcase amateurs or promote van Gogh wannabes."

"She's not an amateur."

Richard sighed and cursed under his breath. "*She?* Surely you didn't offer my services to a woman you just banged."

It pained him to know that wasn't a far stretch from the truth, but he wasn't keen on opening that can of worms. "Nah, nothing like that. I just paid her shop a visit today, and when I saw what she had to showcase, I thought you'd be interested. I never said anything to her about you or R. Fitzgerald Gallery."

"What's the favor, then?"

Grayson took a deep breath. "I was hoping you'd have time tomorrow to swing by and see what she's done. Just take a look."

"And that's it?" Richard asked, clearly expecting more.

"Yeah."

"Gray…" Richard coaxed. "What else is there?"

"Well, if by some chance you don't think her work would fit in your upcoming exhibition, I was…at least…wanting you to buy a few paintings for the studio while you're there."

Richard paused on the other end of the line. A long pause. But Grayson waited. With fingers crossed, he waited.

"Why didn't you just purchase them yourself?"

Grayson opened his mouth and then shut it again. He wasn't prepared for that question. "Um...I figured you'd want to see them first. Make sure they were what you had in mind for the studio. We are equal partners in this venture, right?"

"Sure. I can do that."

He let out a sigh. *Perfect.*

"Which paintings did you have your eyes on?"

"Any of them are fine. I'm not picky. But..." He heard the call of the canvas hanging behind the register. The warm mahogany color of the woman's hair, and the hint of her succulent breasts lured him to the extent that he had to have the work of art resembling Chloe.

"You're not picky but what, Gray?"

"There's a painting right behind the register of her shop. I want that one for myself. But don't tell her it's for me. In fact, don't even bring up my name."

"Here it comes," Richard groaned.

"What?"

"The reason you don't want your name mentioned. Is she some chick you took to bed and promised to call but never did?"

"Richard, please."

"Oh, don't act like that's never happened before. Save your bullshit for someone who doesn't know you as well as

I do."

Grayson drummed his fingers on his leg. He could accept the possibility of Chloe never wanting to see him again, but he couldn't allow her to be left hanging high and dry. He would help her get back on her feet, and with dignity if it was the last thing he did.

"Look. I didn't call to debate my sexual history with you. I just asked you to check out a friend's work, and I'd rather her not know I had anything to do with it. She's a very talented artist, one of the finest I've ever seen, and I want her to believe she made it on her own and not because she was given a handout. Surely, you can understand that."

"Hmm… Impressive."

Grayson furrowed his brow. "What's that supposed to mean?"

"It means I'm awestruck. Grayson Anders wants to do for someone without them 'doing him' first. Has hell frozen over?"

"Screw you."

"I'm serious. This is incredible. You're finally realizing that generosity has its place in your world. And I commend you for it."

Grayson pinched the bridge of his nose. "Does that mean you'll check it out tomorrow?"

"Yes, it does."

Grayson's heart leapt, and he grinned. "Great. I appreciate it. I'll text you the address."

"Sounds good," Richard returned. "Hey, by the way, did you find your mysterious lover and dance partner today?"

Grayson didn't want to lie to his friend. "I'm still working on it."

Richard's cynical laughter followed. "Good luck with that."

****

Monday rolled around, and Grayson was up two hours earlier than normal, simply because he couldn't sleep anymore. He was up most of the night, unable to get a certain amazing woman out of his mind.

He thought of Chloe for hours after he talked to Richard and couldn't wait for the next weeks to pass by, when he would put his next plan into motion. It was going to take some time and some very careful planning to get Chloe to see him in a better light and not as the immature chicken-shit of a man he was yesterday. There were delicate eggshells beneath his feet, and if he didn't play his cards right, he'd never get the chance to prove himself to her.

From here on out, things had to go according to plan, or he could kiss Chloe LaRoche good-bye.

"Ring, dammit!" he commanded the cell phone in his hand while he paced his bedroom. He checked his watch for the third time, wondering why Richard hadn't called yet. Surely, since it was past ten o'clock, Richard should've been to Chloe's by now and seen her paintings. Why hadn't he called?

He threw the phone on the bed and stared at the blank wall across from it, the empty space where his favorite painting would soon hang. He stepped backward until the footboard bumped the back of his knees, and he sat down, envisioning her beautiful self-portrait in front of him. He could imagine closing his eyes to sleep every night with Chloe being the last thing he'd see and the first thing he'd wake up to. His extravagant bedroom, though somewhat plain without curtains, would finally be complete. As far as he was concerned, the only thing that would make his bedroom better would be to have Chloe draped across his bed, in the flesh. For now, he'd take the two-dimensional option on canvas.

While he cogitated further, the phone rang. In haste, he answered it before the second ring.

"Hello?"

"Good morning, Grayson," Richard said with a

peculiar tone in his voice.

He could hear the edginess in his friend's cordial greeting as if something were amiss. "Is there something wrong?"

"Not at all. I just came from Chloe's shop…and I made a few purchases."

Grayson smiled, though his stomach knotted up. "And…"

"And she's going to be one of the featured artists at the Back Bay Boston Exhibit at R. Fitzgerald Gallery. I have a truck picking up all her paintings this afternoon."

A wave of relief washed over him. "Really?"

"Yes, really. She's just like you said, one of the finest artists around. Thanks for the heads-up."

Grayson ran his hand through his hair, still finding it hard to believe the first part of his plan had gone through without a hitch. "No problem. I'm just glad you're going to benefit as well."

"Oh, I can already foresee that," Richard said. "But what I can't predict is why you didn't tell me she was deaf."

Grayson chuckled nervously. "Well, honestly, I didn't want there to be any predisposition on your end. I wanted you to see her work for what it was without feeling like a heel in the event you didn't think her work would make the cut."

"I appreciate that, Gray. But perhaps you can cut the noble-gentleman crap and tell me what part you get to play in all this. Because, frankly, I can't begin to fathom the kind of devious plans you have in store for this woman. Now, granted, she's gorgeous—right up your alley when it comes to picking out the T and A of the world. But she's still deaf, hardly the kind of woman I'd think you'd pursue, if you haven't already."

Grayson came to his feet, a little offended by his friend's implication. "Who said I was pursuing her?"

"You're going to deny it now? Come on, Gray, it's me you're talking to here. I know you better than you know yourself sometimes."

True. He and Richard had too much history together to repudiate that. But now wasn't the time. Not this way. He feared if he told Richard about his involvement with Chloe, it would only hurt her in the end. As much as he'd like to brag about it, he had too much riding on making his strategy work.

"I'm sorry, Richard. I wish I had more to tell you. When it comes to Chloe and me, I'm in the dark as much as you are."

Richard gave a slight grunt on the line. "Still don't believe you, buddy. But, I gotta run. Lots of paperwork to finish before the exhibition opens."

Grayson tried to act surprised. "Right. So, when is it again?"

"Two weeks from today. Why? You planning on attending?"

"Nah," Grayson said. "Not this time."

"You afraid it's too upscale for you?"

"No, I just prefer to be the silent partner in all this."

"Mmm-hmm. I see. Suit yourself."

Grayson hung up the phone, and shoved it in his back pocket. As he mulled over the term silent partner, he grabbed his keys and walked out the door.

****

"You gonna tell me what we're doing here, inconspicuously staking out Chloe's shop like a bunch of snoopin' cops?" Gerry finally asked after about thirty minutes of watching the meter run.

"Just wait," Grayson said from behind his newspaper. "You'll see." He held it up in front of him as if he were reading it, while peeking out from behind it from time to time. He glanced at his watch, figuring an R. Fitzgerald moving truck should be pulling up any second. He didn't care as much about the truck as he did about getting a glimpse of Chloe. He wanted to see her reaction without her realizing she was being watched.

Right on time, a large white truck with fancy blue script passed by and pulled in front of her gallery. Two men exited the vehicle, one with a clipboard, and made their way around the back to the cargo hold, lifting the door open. After a few moments of watching the movers prep the trailer, he saw two women come out and stand on the sidewalk.

Grayson tucked himself behind his newspaper for good measure and peered around it soon after. He didn't recognize one of the women but assumed she was some kind of community interpreter. The other was Chloe, and to his dismay, she looked indifferent to the whole situation. Not at all what he would've expected to see with an R. Fitzgerald Gallery truck sitting in front of her store.

"What's going on?" Gerry asked, his eyes glued to the truck.

"What's it look like?"

Gerry swiveled his head to look Grayson in the eyes, then lifted a single brow in condescension. "Well, as far as I can tell, there are two moving men about to haul Chloe's stuff away."

"Not just any moving truck," Grayson corrected. "An R. Fitzgerald moving truck."

"You mean from R. Fitzgerald Gallery—the R.

Fitzgerald Gallery sitting smack dab in the middle of the elite district of downtown Boston?"

"That would be the one."

Gerry leaned back and watched the movers. "You wouldn't have anything to do with this, would you?"

"As far as you and Chloe are concerned? No."

As the men carrying sealed canvases from Chloe's gallery one by one, Gerry seemed to have picked up on Grayson's Good Samaritan act. "Don't worry, Mr. Anders. Your secret is safe with me."

"I'm confident of that."

"This is good, then. I mean, for Chloe."

"Oh, it's very good," Grayson replied coolly. "Her troubles should be long gone now."

Gerry glanced over his shoulder. "Since when do you care?"

Grayson took a deep breath. "I have no idea."

"Well, I doubt you'll ever know. I've been married twelve years, and I still haven't figured it out. You ever gonna tell Chloe? About this?"

Grayson turned the page of his newspaper, still playing the part of the inconspicuous passenger. "What purpose would it serve?"

Gerry cleared his throat. "It would serve *you*."

"Sure. But, is that really the right way to start a

SILENT PARTNER (The Sweet Version)

relationship? I'd prefer she didn't think she owed me anything."

Gerry shook his head. "Never thought you had it in you."

"Neither did I," Grayson admitted.

"So, what *are* we doing here anyway?"

"Wait for it..." Grayson lowered his newspaper and spied over the top, catching Chloe and her interpreter friend signing back and forth with each other. After a few more hand gestures, he saw Chloe reach out and hug the woman, a huge, bright smile plastered across her face.

Finally.

Grayson slumped in his seat, taking in the beautiful sight. Chloe's genuine smile was the very reaction he'd hoped for and the only thing he needed to see. Nothing more.

"Let's go home, Gerry."

"Yes, sir, Mr. Anders."

****

For days, Grayson had been so preoccupied with Chloe and fixing what he'd screwed up that he hardly realized the weekend had arrived. If not for hearing the loud music his DJ started to play two floors down, he

114

would never have known it was Friday night.

He glanced at his laptop's clock in the bottom corner of his screen: six thirty on the dot.

Normally, he would have been dressed and sitting at the bar with his bartender, Jack, going over drink specials and bouncer placement. Tonight, he wasn't in the mood. All he wanted to do was to continue surfing the web for products dedicated to the deaf. If he wanted Chloe to be his dance partner for his studio, then he had to find some sort of adaptation device that would allow her to hear the slamming bass of the music without blowing everyone else's eardrums out.

After several hours, he did.

He came across Harris Communications, an on-line product site for the deaf and hearing impaired, and to his delight, they sold many different specialty earbuds compatible with all iPhone/iPods/MP3 players. As he clicked around the site reading reviews and various product details, he also came across a Krown Sign Language Translator. It was a cell-phone-size gadget where one could type in a word using the touch screen, and a video would pop up, showing a woman demonstrating the correct way to sign it.

Without hesitation, he clicked the "Add to Cart" button on both the handheld translator and the discreetly sized earbuds and made his purchase. He sat back on his couch, still astonished that these products even existed. Unbeknownst to him, there was a whole new world out there, and he felt quite ashamed for initially thinking Chloe was too far outside of his when, in fact, he was the outsider. For years, she'd been adapting to his world. Now it was time for him to step into hers and walk a mile in her shoes.

He only hoped she wouldn't slam the door in his face when he got there.

After noting the tentative shipping date on his invoice, he shut the laptop and set it aside. He was both excited and nervous for his purchases to arrive, and he hoped that in trying to learn sign language, he wouldn't make any more of an ass of himself than he already had.

A knock at the door interrupted his contemplations. In a trancelike state, he opened the door to find Richard scrolling through emails on his cell.

"Hey." Grayson cleared his head of Chloe and trying to impress her. "What are you doing here?"

"Hello? It's Friday night. We're always here on Friday."

Grayson turned, leaving the door open.

"You all right?" Richard asked, closing it behind him. "You don't look yourself."

"Nah, I'm fine. Just have a lot on my mind, that's all."

Richard cocked his head. "Wouldn't have anything to

do with a certain…artist, would it?"

Grayson froze. "It might."

"Either it does or it doesn't," Richard asserted. "But either way, I'd rather you stop lying about it. We've been friends for too long to start hiding things from each other. So what if you slept with Chloe LaRoche? It's not like—"

"Whoa, whoa, whoa," Grayson interrupted, holding up his hands. "Who said I slept with her?"

Richard hung his head. "All right, if that's the side you're taking, then explain to me how a woman can climb the front of your building, three floors up, where there's no fire escape, and get a good look at you sleeping in your bed?"

"What are you talking about?"

"I was inventorying Chloe's paintings this week, and I came across one in particular. I'm not sure if you've seen it or not, but it's an identical match to your face. Granted, the painting shows a half-naked man lying prone on his bed, but it was strikingly detailed. Now, either she's a regular Peeping Tom, or she knows the ins and outs of you and your bedroom enough to paint you to a T. Considering how preposterous the first one sounds, I'm going with the latter. Here," Richard said, handing over his phone. "Maybe this will jog your memory."

Grayson took the cell from his friend's hand and

gawked at the screen. It appeared she'd painted him sleeping so remarkably well that he noticed she added in the childhood scar on his forearm. When he looked closer, he was able to read the tag beneath it: Adonis at Rest.

Grayson's eyes widened at the title she'd given it, and he blew out his bewilderment in one long breath.

"Yeah," Richard agreed. "That's what I did too."

Speechless, Grayson handed the phone back, the image of that painting burned in his brain.

"Are you still going to stand there and deny sleeping with her?"

"I suppose I can't anymore. However…in my defense, you never asked."

"Yes, I did," Richard argued. "If you'll recall our conversation the other day when you mentioned me stopping to take a look at Chloe's work, I asked you if you offered my services to a woman you just banged."

Grayson nodded. "Exactly. And I told you I didn't. I didn't offer your services to her. That was your question. Not whether or not I slept with her."

"You're splitting hairs here, Gray."

"Call it whatever you want, but I didn't lie to you."

Richard's lips straightened. "Fine. We misunderstood each other. But let's get to the real problem."

"And what would that be?"

"*When* did you sleep with her?" Richard demanded, his arms crossed.

Grayson drew back. "Why does that matter?"

"Because if you say it was this past weekend, then that would mean Chloe is the mysterious woman who won you over and somehow rose to the status of your perfect dance partner despite the fact that she is freakin' deaf! Which, bluntly speaking, seems outright impossible."

Grayson looked away for a moment as empathetic sadness overtook him. "It's possible, because Chloe used to be a dancer before she lost her hearing to a nonmalignant cancer. Bilateral acoustic neuroma. Yeah, I googled it. So as long as the music is loud enough that she can feel it, she can keep the rhythm…and dance."

Richard followed him into the living room and plopped on the couch next to him. "And since you met her at Gyrations, you didn't know the difference before you took her to your bed."

"Basically."

"And you still want Chloe to be your dance partner?"

Grayson stared at his coffee table but didn't really see it. "Yeah."

"Let me guess," Richard added. "She doesn't know how you feel."

"The way I really feel about her? No. But she does

think I'm an asshole."

"Why is that?"

Grayson thought back to the day when he'd walked out on her, the tears in her eyes haunting him since the moment he'd stepped out on the street. "She thinks that because I was. I walked out of her shop with my foot in my mouth and left her crying. I didn't go back. I couldn't face her. I didn't know how. But I do now, and I want to apologize to her."

"So why don't you?"

"I am. I mean, I will. I just have to learn sign language first."

Richard laughed, but when he saw the look on Grayson's face, he stopped. "Oh, you're serious."

"I am. She's got a hold on me, and I can't shake it, Richard. I gotta fix this…one way or another. Starting with the painting."

"Come again?"

"The 'Adonis at Rest.' I don't think she meant to sell it. It's so unlike the other ones, and I think she painted it for herself. I'm betting that since I broke her heart, she's getting rid of it. Tell me I'm wrong."

Richard leaned back on the couch. "I think I might have to agree with you on this one."

Grayson looked at his friend with serious intent. "I

want to buy that painting. No matter what it's going for, I want to buy it. For her. Can you make that happen?"

"Oh, I can make it happen, but you realize it's probably going to cost you. I've got a hunch that piece is going to attract some pretty high bidders given its uniqueness."

"I don't care. Just make sure my bid is always higher."

"If that's what you want."

"Yeah, it's what I want."

"All right, I've had enough of this." Richard slapped Grayson's knee. "Let's go down to the club and have a few. Joyce has a table, and she says you owe her a dance."

Grayson smiled and looked over the clothes he was wearing. "I'll have to change first."

"Well, hurry it up. Joyce has already warned me that we have some celebrating to do."

"Celebrating what?"

"That Grayson Anders has finally lost his heart to a woman."

Chapter Ten

Two weeks later

Richard Fitzgerald, the only man who had believed in her work, walked past a crowd of well-dressed art critics and came toward her.

Chloe's heart skipped. She'd been so nervous in the past weeks about her work being displayed in his beautiful marble-floored and pillared gallery. Now that the day had finally come, she was even more nervous about what Mr. Fitzgerald would think. He seemed impressed with her sensual-style nudes when he'd first seen them hanging in her tiny studio. But now, when they were exhibited among so many other well-known artists' pieces, she feared her paintings paled in comparison.

She felt a hand, firm and reassuring, take hold of hers, and glanced at Evelyn, her interpreter and friend. She gave Chloe a warm smile, letting her know that all would be fine. Chloe was grateful to have her there and smiled back, though inside, she was falling apart.

"Ms. LaRoche," Richard said, reaching for her other

hand and giving it a slight squeeze. He looked between her and Evelyn as if he were unsure to whom he should direct his words. Eventually he let his gaze fall in Chloe's direction so as not to be rude. "I'm so pleased you came. I must admit, I feared you wouldn't."

Chloe looked away. She too hadn't thought she'd make it. Something inside her had urged her to attend, something more insistent than the unrelenting encouragement of her nagging interpreter.

She looked at Evelyn and gave her a nod, allowing her to speak for her.

"Mr. Fitzgerald," Evelyn began. "Chloe wanted you to know she's very grateful for this opportunity. Not many people in her life have given her the time of day, especially once they've found out she is deaf. And when they do present just an inkling of interest in her work, it's usually out of pity and nothing more."

Chloe watched Richard process Evelyn's words—her words. Once he crossed his arms and smiled, she finally relaxed.

"Ms. LaRoche," Richard began, "I've seen many artists come and go in this town. But no one has the innate talent for bringing emotion to their pieces like you have. You've given them a voice, and I'm honored to have given them a home. Well, a temporary one, per se."

Chloe recognized a slight upturn in his grin, as if he knew something she didn't.

"Ah, I see you caught my subtle segue there," Richard replied. "It's the reason I came over to you." He turned briefly, facing the large wall supporting her numerous paintings, and back to her again. "I'm pleased to announce that nine of your paintings have already sold—two of them to that gentleman over there."

Richard nodded to her left toward a tuxedo-clad, middle-aged man standing with a shapely, Marilyn Monroe-type blonde in a striking red evening gown on his arm. As if the man heard his name, he turned and slightly bowed his head.

"That is Mr. James Hollingsworth, Back Bay's most influential architect since Arthur Gilman."

Chloe couldn't believe what she was reading from Richard's lips. To know someone with as much clout as Mr. Hollingsworth had found enough appeal in her work to have purchased them within a few short hours was rather mind-boggling.

"Believe it, Ms. LaRoche," Richard replied as if he'd read her mind. "Your work is in high demand now. With it being showcased here, the demand will only grow." He pointed to one painting in particular. "This one sold for five grand in a matter of minutes."

Chloe swallowed hard as she considered the painting. It was her treasured sleeping Adonis, and even though she'd made the decision to sell it weeks ago, it was difficult to accept that it had actually sold. Her favorite piece had sold to someone who probably wouldn't cherish it the way she had.

"Is something wrong?" Richard asked, glancing between her and Evelyn. "Perhaps the price is too low? I could inform the buyer that he was just overbid if you're not happy with the selling price. I'm pretty sure he'll give you whatever you're looking for."

Chloe didn't know what to say. The last thing she wanted to do was seem ungrateful in front of Mr. Fitzgerald, but it felt as if she were giving up her own child for adoption. Luckily, Evelyn knew enough about how she regarded the unique piece and offered an explanation.

"The selling price is not the issue, Mr. Fitzgerald. The painting you're referring to happens to be a very sentimental piece, and I believe it's just harder for Ms. LaRoche to part with it than she expected."

Chloe stared at the painting, her heart feeling like a ten-pound weight in her chest. She didn't know why she felt so strongly about this painting, but she did. It wasn't as if she'd had a long-term relationship with the man on the canvas or that he'd left her after so many years. In truth, he was nothing more than a one-night stand.

A one-night stand and the next day gone terribly wrong.

It wasn't supposed to be like that. She wasn't supposed to fall for him, and he sure as hell wasn't supposed to find her. He was only meant to be a means for relieving stress, a means to forget her problems and do something crazy and unconventional for one night, and then move on. In the past weeks, she found that moving on was nearly impossible.

For whatever reason, Mr. Gyration had made a huge impression on her, especially after he found her the next day, and she couldn't rid his memory from her mind. Reminiscing on those tender moments caused a strange ache in her heart, the same one she'd suffered the second he turned his back on her and walked out the door. Even now, after more than two weeks, the pain of his departure hurt as deeply as the day it happened. She doubted it would go away anytime soon.

A hand touched her shoulder, interrupting the self-pitying stupor she was in.

"Ms. LaRoche, I can't help but notice that your 'Adonis at Rest' is quite different from the others. If you don't mind me asking, from whom did you get your inspiration?"

Chloe feigned her best pleasant smile and began signing. Evelyn chimed in with, "He was a man from my recent past, but someone I barely knew. I just woke up one morning and had to paint him. An impulse."

As she finished her explanation, a look of compassion entered Mr. Fitzgerald's eyes as if he understood her pain. "Realize all sales are final. But I know the buyer personally…so if you'd rather not sell it…"

She waved him off, knowing it was better for her heart to let it go. Selling the painting would be a necessary step to moving on.

"She'll be fine, Mr. Fitzgerald," Evelyn said, taking hold of Chloe's shoulders. "Sometimes it's just hard to let go. She'll get used to it."

"Of course," he replied, nodding once. "I'll give you some time. Again, I'm so pleased you came, Ms. LaRoche. Feel free to look around."

Chloe watched him leave to join another small group of people admiring a brightly colored abstract painting. A feeling of loss weighed her down. She should be happy about her successful sales, enjoying the day for what it was. Not many artists got the chance to be represented by R. Fitzgerald Gallery, or to be noticed by such respectable men like Mr. James Hollingsworth.

All she really wanted was to have Mr. Gyrations'

respect. To go back in time and relish the way he looked at her with longing, to see the high regard in which he once held her, before he found out the truth. She wasn't ashamed of being deaf, but she certainly wished she could've done things differently. Perhaps if she hadn't jumped into his bed so quickly, they could've at least remained friends.

Chloe looked at Evelyn, grateful for her presence. She touched her mouth with her fingertips and laid it in her open left hand.

"You don't have to thank me, Chloe. I'm honored to be here with you." Evelyn lifted her chin. "Your Adonis, no matter how godlike he is, was still a shallow chicken-shit. But look at it this way. You just made a pretty penny off that bastard. At least he was good for something."

Chloe cringed and signed, "And that isn't shallow?"

"You deserve to be a little superficial. Now let's forget about him and meet some people who actually deserve to know you. Like Mr. Hollingsworth over there."

Chloe glanced at the sharply dressed, handsome man and rolled her eyes. She knew she wasn't going to get out of this one with Evelyn in her company, and, for no other reason than to show appreciation toward Mr. Fitzgerald for all he'd done for her, she sucked it up and mingled with the public.

****

Grayson practiced his apology to Chloe over and over, as many times as he could. He wanted it near flawless. He'd visited Brigit Sullivan, Gerry's sister, on several occasions, learning the basics of sign language, and he used his portable translator in between lessons.

Brigit had taught him how to sign each letter of the alphabet first, and then, once he perfected that, he learned the fundamentals like "please" and "thank you," "my name is...," and "what time is it?" But knowing the bare bones wasn't enough. He wanted to speak to Chloe in her language. He wanted to give her an honest apology in a way she'd appreciate. He wanted to prove, by being as proficient as he could with signing, that he was truly willing to go the distance with her and get to know her on a deeper level than just great sex.

It was nearly killing him to go this long without it, though—without Chloe. She'd been by far the best he'd ever had, and just thinking about the possibility of touching her again aroused him.

Focus, Grayson.

He willed those thoughts away and kept to his lessons. Every day he practiced. From the time he woke to the moment the sun set again. Tonight was going to be the night he'd put his words into motion—literally.

As he tried one more time in front of his mirror, he knew everything was riding on this one apology. He was nervous. And he hated it.

It wasn't like him to fret over things. He *was* a perfectionist, through and through, but when something as important as impressing a special woman was in his plans, he refused to cut corners.

He'd made so many calls in the past week, to caterers, to candle shops, to his own employees. Everything seemed to be lined up for the grand finale. The only thing he was waiting for was a phone call that would tell him whether or not this was all a go.

Grayson paced his bedroom floor, stopping a few times to check his tux in the mirror. As he figured, it hadn't changed any since the last time he inspected it. He glanced at the wall across from the bed, eyeing the canvas that used to hang above Chloe's register. Ever since Richard had brought it home, he couldn't walk out of his room without admiring it. But today, he looked at the painting of the dark-haired beauty and his stomach fluttered. He had butterflies, of all things—butterflies that made him half-sick.

As he laid his hand on his stomach, his cell rang. He

jerked it out of his pocket and checked the display. Richard.

"Hey."

"I have good news," Richard said. "She's agreed to meet."

Grayson exhaled. "What did you tell her?"

"I told her what you asked me to say. That a colleague of mine was very impressed with her work and wanted to meet her."

"And you told her you would pick her up for dinner?"

"Yes, Gray. I told Chloe everything you wanted me to say and nothing more."

Grayson sat on the edge of the bed, brainstorming through every possible flaw in his little scheme. "Was she suspicious?"

"Why should she be?"

"I don't know. I'm just…"

"Gray," Richard said, stopping him short. "Everything's going to be fine. I told her my driver would pick her up at eight sharp. So, she's expecting someone to be there. It better be you."

"Don't worry. I'll be there."

"You'd better be. My ass is on the line here, you know."

"I know," Grayson said. "I won't let you down."

****

Grayson sat in the backseat of the black stretch limo he'd rented for the night, his heart pounding like a bass drum. Never had he been so tense about a woman or the moment leading up to a date. Even on his first prom date, he was Mr. Joe Cool. Tonight, he felt like the geeky teenager who'd finally gotten the popular girl to cave and say yes to him.

He looked out the tinted window at the passing street lights and the eclectic night life of Beacon Hill. It was part of the reason he loved Boston so much, with its quaint little restaurants and unusual boutiques tucked within the eccentric nightspots and clubs. There was something for everyone there.

But all Grayson wanted was Chloe LaRoche.

He wanted her so badly, he could taste it. Absently, he licked his lips, imagining her sweet mouth on his. He remembered the sensation of her kiss, the way she tilted her head slightly as though she were sinking into it.

His fancy silver-and-black-striped ascot suddenly felt too tight around his neck. He slipped his fingers beneath his tuxedo collar and pulled on it, wishing he could lower his window. He needed fresh air, but he needed his plan to come off without a hitch even more. If he rolled down the window, he'd risk Chloe seeing him prematurely. He didn't want that to happen until she was inside the limo and secured within a moving vehicle.

Suddenly, the inside window separating him from the driver opened. "We're coming up on Charles Street, sir."

Grayson tried to act like he was in complete control of himself. He uttered a deep, composed version of "thank you" and slid far away from the door.

And waited.

He had no idea how fast his heart could beat until he felt the limo come to a halt.

Chapter Eleven

Chloe stepped out of her shop and onto the red brick pavement, dressed to the hilt in a little black dress, excited for this grand opportunity. When Mr. Fitzgerald had told her about his colleague wanting to meet her, he never said it was going to be such a formal affair. She could only assume he was another one of those Mr. James Hollingsworth types who had money to burn and a lifetime supply of matches.

As the driver circled the front of the shiny black limo, she took a moment to calm herself. A few deep breaths did wonders for her nerves, and when the driver opened the door for her, she was ready.

She stepped inside and sat down, the size of its spacious interior overwhelming her. The only time she'd ever traveled in a limo was for a friend's wedding, and there were so many people crammed into it, the vehicle resembled a clown car.

In the far corner of the vehicle, a man sat in the dark shadow. She waved to him, assuming it was Mr. Fitzgerald, and wished Evelyn could've come with her. It disappointed her that Evelyn had a former engagement. Hopefully, it wouldn't be a long ride to the restaurant.

As soon as the limo pulled away from the curb, Mr. Fitzgerald slid closer to her seat and flipped on the interior lights. Only it wasn't Mr. Fitzgerald.

Her first impulse was to run away. But she was in a moving vehicle.

Trapped.

Anger flooded her, and an uncomfortable heat rose up her neck. She didn't know whether to be mad at Mr. Fitzgerald for tricking her or furious at…at…whatever his freakin' name was!

Desperation got the better of her, and she reached for the handle of the door and tried it anyway. It was locked, which was just as well because she probably would've jumped out of the limo regardless of its speed.

She'd always wondered how she'd feel if she ever saw Mr. Gyration again. If she ever ran into the man who'd treated her so rudely. So coldly. Now, though completely unprepared for it, she found out.

Chloe glared back at him, seething like a helpless, caged animal. And she did what any normal irritated Bostonian would've done. She flipped him the bird.

****

Grayson didn't know too many signs in sign language, but he certainly knew that one. He did his best to hide the humor he found in her obscene gesture and scooted closer to her.

As he expected, she inched farther away, all the way against the door. What he hadn't predicted was her grabbing the hem of her short black dress and jerking it down her thighs as if his only reason for meeting with her was to come on to her.

"*What do you want?*" Chloe signed crossly.

Grayson assumed she'd ask that, and he'd practiced the answer weeks ahead of time. He held his hands in front of him for a few seconds, trying to remember the correct string of gestures. "*I want to apologize to you.*"

Chloe's brows rose. She was unable to hide her surprise with him signing, and he was glad to see he had her full attention. He tried again. "*I do not deserve much from you, but will you at least give me the chance to apologize?*" At the end of his question, he circled his open hand on his chest, depicting a sincere "*please.*"

She glanced out her window, pondering. She clearly wanted to give him a piece of her mind and was fighting the urge not to. When she finally looked back in his direction, the hard lines of her face relaxed, and an angelic beauty reemerged before him. Reluctantly, she nodded.

Relief washed over him. He touched his mouth and let his hand fall into his other hand, gesturing his appreciation in the form of *"thanks."*

Okay, Grayson…just like you practiced. Don't mess it up.

Again he lifted his hands in front of him, readying himself for his big speech. He hated that his hands trembled. There was no way to hide his nervousness in front of her. For the first time, he felt vulnerable. A fraction of a man.

Still, he trudged forward.

He began with an introduction, since they'd never exchanged names. He patted his chest and tapped the first two fingers of both hands together. *"Hello. My name is Grayson Anders."* He took more care in finger-spelling his name, making sure he accounted for every letter correctly. *"And I am an asshole."*

Immediately, Chloe brought her hand up to her mouth to stifle her laughter. He smiled back, pleased that he'd gotten the reaction he wanted, and pressed forward.

"From the moment I first saw you, I knew you were someone I had to meet. And from the moment you danced with me, I knew I had found the only dance partner for me. For years, I had searched. No one had made me feel so sure of myself as you had. It was the reason I

pursued you so adamantly. When I walked into your shop, I saw the real woman behind the passion. You moved me. You touched a place within me, once guarded by walls of wariness. But when I found out you were deaf, I was scared. And selfish. I forgot how connected we were. All I could think about was how my world had been turned upside down, never thinking it was I who barged into yours."

Grayson closed his eyes, trying to get through the last part. He knew it would prove to be the most difficult, for he was about to lay bare his soul to a woman, one he risked losing if he didn't say the right things.

He felt a touch on his leg and glanced down to find her slender hand on his knee. He looked at her, his heart pounding as their gazes caught and held.

Grayson swallowed back his rising fears and continued. *"Being away from you has made me realize how much I need you. How much I need you in my life. I know we have a language barrier, but I've been working hard to amend that, as you can see."*

He saw pity in her eyes now. It wasn't what he'd planned for, but he'd take sympathy if it kept her attentive.

Gathering his bravado once more, he rehearsed the last part of his practiced apology in his head. *Shit.* He forgot the sign for *"willing."*

Panic struck him, and his mouth went dry. How could he forget the most important part? He'd rehearsed this speech so many times in the past weeks that he could almost do it in his sleep. Behind the safety of closed doors, it came easily. Now he was drawing a complete blank.

Desperate to finish his words exactly the way he'd prepared them, he spun around on his seat and pulled out his translator from his suit pocket, hiding it behind his back.

Frantically, he typed in the word and waited for the woman to appear on the screen with the sign. She touched her chest with an open hand and moved it away from her in a single leaping motion.

Dammit, I knew that. Frustrated with himself, he pocketed the device. But as he turned back around, he almost bumped heads with Chloe, who'd come close enough to look over his shoulder.

As they stared at each other, their noses nearly touching, it was obvious Chloe had seen the gadget. Automatically, his mouth fell open, and he closed it just as quickly. It was only natural for him to want to use words, but he swore he wasn't going to take the easy route with her. She deserved more.

He slipped his fist between them with his thumb up, careful not to touch her in any way, and made two circular motions on his chest for the word "*sorry.*"

She glanced down at his heartfelt signal and signed back, "*Why?*"

Grayson tensed. He didn't know how to sign his answer. He racked his brain, trying to remember bits and pieces of the sign language he *did* know.

Nothing.

Chloe raised her open hand to her face and tapped the side of her fingers to her chin, motioning him to just speak the words.

"*Too easy,*" he signed in return.

Chloe closed her eyes and hung her head slightly. Her brows furrowed and her lips thinned. He knew that look. She was talking herself into something. But what, he couldn't come close to guessing.

"What. If," she said word by word, "I. Spoke. Too?"

Grayson didn't mean to let his mouth gape open, but it dropped beyond his control. She'd just spoken to him! More importantly, he was able to hear a voice—her voice. It was a bit monotone, but it was there, and he was thrilled. "You can talk?"

She nodded. "I don't like to, though."

Grayson sensed her pulling away, embarrassed, and he reached for her. "Why? Why don't you like to speak?"

She grimaced as she tried so desperately to enunciate each word in her reply. "Because I know it doesn't sound…" She paused, glancing away, "as good to the hearing ears of the world."

"You're wrong. Your voice is the most beautiful sound I've ever heard. You should never be ashamed of it."

She shrugged him off.

"I'm serious." He reached up to touch her cheek. "I'm honored you would share the sound of your voice with me. It took a lot of courage for you to do that."

"No more than you trying to sign for me. I'm just trying to get used to being deaf in a hearing world. As much as I've learned to accept my deafness and adapt to it, there's still a part of my old life that I can't let go of. And you're the first person who's allowed me to hold on to both."

Grayson smiled, hearing her speak to him in a more fluent manner. How idiotic he was to think she couldn't speak. He should've known better than to assume every deaf person was also mute. Given the fact she retained her hearing for most of her life, it would only be logical for her to still be able to formulate words.

As he sat before her, he couldn't remember being so happy. Their so-called language barrier had been slightly removed, and it seemed she'd even let down her guard. Bridging that gap was a huge advancement in their relationship, if he could actually call it one, and this was as good a time as any to take another daunting step.

"I have something for you," he stated. "Something else I think you wanted to hold on to." He slid across to the other seat and patted the place beside him. "Please."

Chloe slowly joined him and looked in the direction he was staring, a lingering apprehension still present. Sitting on the floor of the limo, resting against the seat, parallel to theirs, was a large present wrapped in yellow paper and an oversized matching bow.

"Go on," he urged.

He watched her slide to the edge of the seat, her dress inching up her thighs. *Knock it off*, he warned, dragging his eyes from the sight of her shapely legs. *Baby steps, you idiot.* He might have convinced his eyes to look away, but the rest of his body didn't care for the idea. Beneath his tuxedo pants, there was a lot of opposition rising.

He shifted in his seat, nonchalantly covering his lap with an arm, and waited patiently for her to unwrap the gift. She was methodical in removing the bow, as if breaking it would be bad luck. Then, in one swift movement, she tore the corner of the paper away, revealing what was underneath.

He could've sworn he heard her gasp, but it was so low he could've more likely dreamt it. He could have yearned for it so strongly that his ears invented the beautiful sound. When her hands ripped away the rest of the paper, he knew he'd struck a chord regardless. As she gawked at her "Adonis at Rest" painting, her face glowed and her chocolate-brown eyes were bright with excitement.

She looked at him and back at the canvas again, her lips slightly parted as if in wonder. "*You* bought it?" she asked as she signed simultaneously.

He could still detect her apprehension for speaking, and that was fine by him. He didn't need long orations from her. He was just glad she tried.

"Yes," Grayson admitted proudly. "Richard Fitzgerald is a good friend of mine. And he called me the minute he saw it. Now I know what you're thinking," he blurted. "That because of my relationship with Richard, you're being featured in his gallery. But nothing could be further from the truth. All I did was tell him where he could find you. Richard is a very particular man and doesn't exhibit anyone at R. Fitzgerald Gallery if they don't meet his standards. And trust me, they are extremely high."

Chloe took hold of the painting with both hands and stared at it for a long time, focusing on the man sleeping in the soft pastel sheets. There was reverence in the way she gazed at it, and Grayson merely waited in silence, giving her all the time she needed.

He saw a tear slip from her eye and roll down her cheek.

He sat up straighter and caught the tear with his thumb, turning her face toward him. "Don't cry, Chloe. I didn't do this to hurt you."

"I'm not hurting inside," Chloe explained, combining her voice with hand signals. "I'm touched. This is the sweetest thing anyone has ever done for me."

He brushed her hair away from her face, taking in this moment. She was talking with him. Even though she spoke with her hands as well, it was amazing to watch her do it so adeptly. He was mesmerized by what she could do: read lips, sign, paint, dance. And now added to that list was talk.

It was a blessed moment, indeed. Even better was knowing he could remain close to her, touch her, and she would no longer try to escape. He cradled her face, stroking her cheek ever so softly. "These are good tears?"

"Yes."

Her reply came out in a sensual whisper, its erotic flare tickling him in all the wrong places. It was almost impossible for him to restrain himself. All he wanted to do was take her in his arms and kiss her just like the night they'd met, without reservation or shame. He wanted it so badly that it seemed like an eternity since he'd tasted her. That if he decided to kiss her lips right now, there was a good chance it would feel like the first time all over again.

He thought back to their first kiss in the stairwell of his building when she'd turned, measured him up for a few seconds, and pulled his face down to hers with both hands.

He recalled the uncertain exploration of her tongue, and how damn hard it was to just stand there and let her test the waters. Torture him.

If it hadn't been for the two shot glasses in his hand, he probably wouldn't have let her kiss him that way. But every man had his limits, and when she slanted her mouth over his, he remembered kissing those boundaries good-bye and never looking back.

What was holding him back now?

He didn't know. He'd always heard that one could look in the eyes of a woman and just know it was meant to be. He'd never really understood how that could be possible until now. As he gazed at her, he found comfort there, and he was perfectly content to drown in her eyes.

It surprised him to think he could be this compassionate, this sensitive, because, truth be told, it wasn't his style. Being fancy-free and self-centered was always his approach toward life, and it was safe.

That was before Chloe. She came along and wreaked havoc over everything he stood for, and it suited him just fine. As long as he had her friendship, he could survive in this crazy new world he'd stepped into.

Realizing how long he'd been staring at her, he resisted the urge to kiss her. With a serious expression, he signed the last practiced part of his speech, the simplest of his words. *"Can you forgive me?"*

Immediately, she smiled and began signing with excitement, her inarticulate words breaking as she spoke. "Of course, I forgive you. How could I not, especially after all you've done. The painting, learning to sign, and this," she said, reaching into his coat jacket and pulling out his pocket translator. "I know how much this costs."

"I didn't care."

"And I know how much you spent on the canvas. Mr. Fitzgerald told me how much it went for. You really shouldn't have."

Grayson shook his head modestly. "After how I treated you...yes, I had to. It was the least I could do. Besides, I couldn't get you out of my head. I knew the moment I walked away, I was making the biggest mistake of my life. But I'm a guy with a lot of pride, and it takes a lot to admit I was wrong. And I'm so glad I did."

He looked down at the translator in her hands and recognized there was still so much to sift through, so much to spell out. Doing so would mean exposing his innermost thoughts, where his heart would be completely susceptible to breaking.

He took a deep breath of courage and told her his desires. "You painted me with such contentment on my face, and I realized it was the only time I ever felt fulfilled.

When I woke, the morning after I spent the night in your arms, I was truly satisfied. You gave me that sense of peace. Now, I know I don't deserve to ask anything more of you than what I've already taken, but if you give me a chance, I can be the man you painted on that canvas."

Chloe stared at him. He endured the warmth of her concentrated focus, and his silky ascot started to choke him again as he waited for her answer.

She leaned closer, and it nearly stole the breath from his lungs. He swallowed, contending with the sweet smell of her perfume invading his nose and the overwhelming proximity of her mouth to his. He glanced down at her lips. In his opinion, they were far too strained, not the kind of lips that were intent on a kiss.

She was going to turn him down. He knew it. She was only inching closer because she was setting him up for what was to come. She was going to take his heart in her talented little hands and drop it by the wayside. How could he blame her? He didn't deserve another chance, and he was damn stupid to have even asked.

He closed his eyes, the torment too strong. Over the pounding of his heart, her voice finally broke through. "Kiss me now...talk later."

****

Chloe saw Grayson's eyes flash open right before she took his lips. Ever since she'd set foot in the limo, angry or not, she wanted to kiss those delicious lips. It took everything she had to restrain herself, especially with him dressed in that swanky tuxedo. Then, after discovering all the trouble he'd gone through to make this night happen and all the lessons he'd taken in order to communicate with her... How could she not want to kiss him?

All this time, she'd assumed he was nothing more than a man who cared only for himself, a womanizing bastard who thought the world revolved around him. And here he'd been secretly planning and preparing, buying paintings and learning sign language just so he could say he was sorry.

For now, she didn't worry about the past. She was too preoccupied with stroking his irresistible tuxedo-clad chest while his strong hands ran over her hips.

She'd missed this. She'd missed the masculine heat radiating from under his clothes, the solid muscles beneath her palms, and the intensity of his passionate kisses. If Grayson Anders was anything, he was a hot, sexy bundle of male virility and a damn good kisser.

He pulled her onto his lap and dove to her neck, planting kisses all the way down to her shoulder. His fingers hooked into the spaghetti strap on her dress and pulled it aside, and that was when the limo came to a halt.

They both froze, realizing the position they sat in: He was reclined far back against the seat, and somehow, she was straddling his lap, her legs bent beneath her.

Grayson cleared his throat. "It appears we're here."

She tried to nonchalantly lift herself from his thighs, but his hands cupped her bottom, stopping her. His grip on her was hard and demanding. If it weren't for the warmth of his body, she might have flirted with the idea of him being made of cool marble.

"The night isn't over, you know."

She tried to peer through the dark tint of the window.

"We're at the club," he confessed. "There's something I want to show you."

Chloe gave him a brilliant smile, revealing her eagerness to go wherever he wanted to take her. But it was difficult to remove herself from him, especially when he was already in the most tempting of positions. Sprawled across the seat in his tux was fast becoming one of her favorite images of him. He reminded her of an ad for Hugo men's cologne, all suave and wickedly handsome in his evening attire, his face newly shaved, his eyes tumultuous and brooding.

She rested her forearms on his shoulders, smoothed the hair at the base of his neck with both hands, and bent to kiss him. It was meant to be a parting kiss, a gentle peck on the lips, but he changed that real quick.

He embraced her, drawing his hands higher up her sides as he deepened the kiss. His tongue slid along hers, and she was helpless to stop him from exploring her in every way. Between knowing where to touch and how to kiss, he was the best. And it was difficult to keep her own hands from loosening his tie and ripping his shirt off.

She pulled away abruptly. She had to, or else, given their history, she'd never stop.

He smiled, proud as a peacock and just as breathless as she was. After a few more calming pants, he glanced toward the passenger door behind them. "We should probably go in."

She couldn't agree more. She was already able to cross "one-night stand" with this guy off her list, and "sex in the back of a limo" wouldn't look any better.

She grabbed her clutch from the seat, and the door immediately opened. The driver waited like a Queen's Guard at Buckingham Palace, but without the flashy red coat. Grayson stepped out behind her, holding the large canvas. He exchanged words with the driver and shook hands, discreetly passing a tip. After that, he gestured toward his club's front entrance, where a single bouncer stood behind burgundy velvet ropes.

"Ms. LaRoche. Mr. Anders," the tall, broad-shouldered man said as he opened the door for them.

"Gerry," Grayson replied. "Glad to see you accepted my offer."

"What can I say, mate? Getting paid to punch egocentric pigs like yourself in the face on a nightly basis is hard to pass up. No offense to you, Mr. Anders."

"None taken."

Chloe was awestruck as she recognized her personal cabbie. *"You two know each other?"* she signed.

Grayson ushered her inside. "That's story for another day, wouldn't you agree, Gerry?"

"Indeed, Mr. Anders. Enjoy your evening, Ms. LaRoche."

When Chloe walked through the door, she was surprised to see a spacious dance floor, a spinning disco ball and all its glorious effects, a few dozen tables, and a long bar—all empty. There wasn't a soul in the place, and it was Friday night.

"I gave everyone the night off. Well," he amended, glancing back at the door. "Almost everyone."

He watched as she touched her forehead and slid her fingertips off her brow, forming the letter Y with her thumb and pinky.

"Because this night is for you. For us."

Chloe gazed out across the floor, confused.

"Not here," he said, shaking his head. "Upstairs. Second floor."

With her curiosity climbing, she turned toward the hallway she remembered from the last time she was here, and lifted her brows.

"Yeah, the stairwell," he directed with a quick nod. "Though, I'm afraid you'll have to get the keys from my pocket." He held the canvas out in front of him, proving his hands were once again full.

She sauntered up to him, playing his little game. Just like old times, she didn't reach in and get his keys. She fumbled around, grazing him repeatedly on purpose. She couldn't say it was all for him. There was a bit of selfishness in her actions.

"Chloe," he warned, closing his eyes. "The keys. I beg you."

Like he asked, she drew them out, but not without one last brush on the way out.

"Second floor," he reminded her.

Together they walked toward the far wall, through the hallway. She unlocked the first door and held it open for him, then followed him up the first flight of stairs.

Her gaze fell naturally to his lower half, taking in the way his trousers fit him perfectly. They weren't as revealing as the tight leather pants he once wore, but given how terribly sexy he looked in that ensemble, with his broad shoulders and narrow hips, she knew his tux had to have been altered by a personal tailor.

He turned around abruptly with a shit-eating grin on his face. "You like what you see?"

Chloe raised and lowered her open palms alternately, conveying a wishy-washy maybe, and climbed the rest of the stairs ahead of him. When she got to the landing, she stood at the door, anxious. She'd never been on the second floor before and couldn't imagine what he wanted to show her.

He leaned the painting against the wall and took the keys from her hand. As he unlocked the door, he brought her into his arms and gazed into her eyes. "I hope you like it."

He opened the door for her and held it. Down the hall, she saw a bright glow coming from one of the rooms, a golden light flickering against the corridor walls.

"Go on."

Excited to see what was causing such a display, she walked in, though tentative in her steps. At the first door, her mouth fell open. Inside the room were hundreds of lit candles, all different heights and widths, scattered about. Some were fitted in glorious candelabras, some in fancy jars, and some were merely tea lights lighting the perimeter where floor-to-ceiling mirrors hung on the walls. It was obvious from the open space of the room and the type of hardwood on the floor that it was a dance studio. But in the center of it all sat a table for two, complete with two tapers, a white tablecloth, shiny white china, and gleaming crystal glasses. Sitting on the edge of the table was a silver ice bucket with a bottle of champagne.

She felt his presence behind her, but he didn't speak until she turned around to face him. "What do you think?"

She opened her fingers in front of her face in a counterclockwise motion, ending at her lips, an unmistakable emotion in her face.

"You really think it's beautiful?" he asked.

She turned to take it all in again. The reflection of the many flickering candles was a breathtaking sight, but nothing could've come close to seeing herself in the mirror. It had been a long time since she'd stood in front of a tall panel mirror, and it all came pouring back. The excitement, the splendor, the rush of staring back at a dancer.

Grayson clasped her shoulders as they gazed at each other in the mirror. "I know how you lost your hearing and what you had to give up because of it. But whoever told you you couldn't dance was a fool. I've seen you dance. I've danced *with* you." He spun her to face him. "You can do this."

Fear took hold of her. There was no way could she dance anymore. She'd only make a fool of herself trying. The only way she could possibly dance was if she could feel its vibrations, and that meant turning the bass volume up to extraordinary levels. At the expense of blowing out everyone's eardrums, she wasn't going to dance, at least not in a studio in front of people. She'd continue to dance in the privacy of her own home.

He lifted her face in his hands. "I know you want to dance."

She clenched her jaw, frustrated that he was pushing this difficult memory on her. If she could accept it, why couldn't he? Defensively, she started to sign all kinds of reasons why this couldn't happen and why it was best for her to walk away. But she was gesturing too quickly for him to keep up.

"Whoa, whoa," he said, catching her flailing hands. "You're going too fast. I can't understand you."

With tears stinging her eyes, she closed them tightly, wishing the hard lump in her throat would go away. She hated to cry about this, because she'd cried longer than she could remember and shed more tears than she could count.

Not anymore. She refused to weep over her hearing loss. This was a hard fact of life and there was nothing that could be done about it. Her cancer was operable, thank God, but her deafness was irreversible. It was a small price to pay for being alive.

He shook her gently, and when she opened her eyes, she found him holding an iPod and a string of earbuds. She wanted to roll her eyes at him. "*I'm deaf,*" she signed sarcastically.

"This isn't what you think," he contended, untangling the wires. "Did you or did you not dance with me downstairs at the club?"

Again, her frustration blasted out of her, her hands going a mile a minute. He grabbed them, ignoring her excuses.

"You can say all you want, but you were able to dance with me because you felt the vibrations. And these," he said, holding up the tiny earphones, "will let you feel those."

She glared at him, her hands on her hips.

"Don't look at me like that. Just try. For me."

Chloe sighed and grabbed the earbuds, but it was only to prove him wrong. While she inserted the plugs in her ears, he sifted through song choices.

"Ah, David Bisbal, here we go, one of your favorites."

He smiled devilishly and strapped the iPod to her upper arm. "Yeah, I know he's your favorite. Course, everyone on Charles Street knows it too."

She shrugged, unimpressed, and waited for something to happen. She watched as he fixed the settings on the side, and immediately, she felt a sensation in her ears, vibrations similar to the ones she'd feel when her music was turned up. Grayson didn't seem to be irritated with it. It looked as if he couldn't hear it at all.

Before she could ask the next logical question, he held his finger up and ran over to the corner of the room, where his laptop and a Bose speaker were set up. He made a few clicks and hit the Enter button, his hips already starting to gyrate.

He looked at her and smiled as if he'd performed some great feat, and sauntered toward her, an obvious rhythm in his steps as he tore off his tuxedo jacket and threw it on the chair. Snaking his left arm around her back, he pulled her firmly against him and grabbed her right hand.

"I've programmed my stereo to receive your FM transmitter frequency. So what you feel in those, I hear the same from the speaker."

She bit her lip, uncertain of herself and her capabilities. She didn't want to disappoint him, especially after all he'd gone through to set up this little experiment, but she also didn't want to disappoint herself. If she couldn't dance at the caliber she used to, it would be like going through the initial pang of failure all over again.

"You ready?"

She tried to shove away all the doubt and nodded.

"Hang on tight, sweet thing. I'm about to sweep you off your feet again."

His nostalgic warning was so cliché, but she had to smile at his confidence. It was one of the reasons she'd fallen for him a month ago and why she was falling for him yet again.

He moved into her, pushing his pelvis against hers, rocking to the beat without moving his feet. Once he demonstrated the timing of the song with his hips, he nodded once and stepped back, leading her into the first steps of the dance.

With his arm firmly around her back, he whirled her about, never taking his eyes from hers. Their gazes locked as they moved in flawless rhythm. She was doing it. And doing it well.

He smiled with her, sharing in her joy. "There you go. Feel it. Be it. Own it."

His words coerced a courage within her she'd long since forgotten, and no one had been able to reach this repressed side of her, save Grayson. It was truly inspirational to think he knew so much about her without really knowing her. He was a godsend. A person sent to her to remind her of how much she loved to dance and that she could if she just tried.

All night, they danced together, never tiring. She was the happiest she'd been in a long time. His smile remained all the while, and in his dark-amber eyes, she saw pride.

After what seemed like hours of stepping, twisting, and sweating, he dipped her over his forearm. And she didn't mind when he dragged his hand down her neck and over her chest. Like last time, his thumb and pinky grazed her breasts before he reached the flat of her stomach and stood her up. He gazed deep into her eyes as they both caught their breaths.

"You're amazing. There's no one who can dance with me like you."

Chloe blushed at his flattering compliment.

"I'll make a deal with you," he said, his tawny eyes full of anticipation. "I'll keep learning sign language if you'll be my partner when I open this studio next week."

She couldn't believe what he asked. And she sure as heck couldn't contain her excitement. She hugged him tightly around the neck, and he swung her around.

When he set her back on her feet, he paused and prepared his hands. "While I was learning to sign, I was told every deaf person has a name sign, specific only to them. This is the one I made up for myself." He formed the letter "G" for Grayson and danced it across his palm. "What do I call you?"

Impressed with his knowledge, Chloe straightened her face and lifted her own hands in front of her. Methodically, she curved her hand in the shape of a "C," held it to her lips momentarily, then crossed her open hands, fanning them away from her face. Immediately following, she held up two fingers on her left hand and placed them in her right fist.

****

Grayson didn't know much about sign language, but he knew she'd just demonstrated a "C" for Chloe and the sign for "silent partner" as her name sign.

That was music to his ears.

THE END

If you enjoyed this book by Renee Vincent, please consider leaving an honest review. Reviews not only give credibility to an author's work, they also help other readers find quality books worth reading.

The Start of Something Good

Jamett & Joseph Series, Book One

Renee Vincent
writing as
Gracie Lee Rose

Chapter One

"You're such a jerk!"

The malicious tone and volume of a woman's complaint caused my head to turn in the direction of the chaos a few doors down the hall of my apartment complex. After whipping her scarf around her neck in finality, the angered woman marched down the corridor. A man, who I assume was the jerk in question, pursued her. At this moment, I realized their argument was not meant for my eyes or ears. The guy showed up for the fight in nothing but a towel. His weapons of choice were bare hands, bare feet, and dripping-wet, wavy brown hair. His muscled chest and arms boasted the remnants of a golden summer tan, even in late November.

I rolled my eyes. How was it possible that men still

looked divine in winter, while we women have to make an occasional visit to the tanning salon so we don't appear pasty white? Sure, some of us tried rockin' the pale skin look of the Twilight vampire craze, but it never seemed to catch on with the male population. They still preferred their women toned and tanned, or at least that was my conclusion given no man had yet to fall head over heels for me.

"How can I be a jerk for trying to help you forget about your horrible day?" he asked, grasping the woman's arm and tugging her back. Thankfully, he was oblivious to me standing three doors down.

"No, you're a jerk because *you* tried to forget about *my* horrible day by coming on to me," the girl corrected.

The woman then looked past the man's bare shoulder and suddenly took notice of my presence. The minute our eyes met, heat flushed my entire body. I quickly averted my attention and pretended not to notice their public tiff, fiddling with my keys to find the right one for locking up. I didn't know what angered her more—the fact that I had taken an interest in their argument or that I had seen her boyfriend in a state of near nakedness.

I half expected her to call me out. Instead, she went back to berating the guy. From where I stood, I had established him as a normal, sexually-active, heterosexual male. It also bears mentioning that he looked very fine in his bathroom apparel.

"I came to you because I needed you, Joseph."

Ah, the jerk in the towel had a name. Not sure why I made a mental note of it, but I did.

"And I'm still here," he concluded, spreading his arms wide. "You're the one who's leaving."

Clearly, the man was not in tune with the proverbial emotional needs of modern day women. If I were keeping score, he'd have lost a point for that little sarcastic remark. However, his choice of morning attire kept the tally in his favor.

"You just don't get it, do you?" she barked back, slamming her hands upon her hips. "You think everything can be solved with a song or sex."

A song? Now this just got a little more interesting.

"You didn't like what I wrote?" he asked.

With my eyes still buried in the ring of keys clutched in my gloved hands, I couldn't help but notice the slight hint of sadness in Joseph's voice. My heart longed to sneak a peek at him, another potential point in his favor should I see a pitiful expression of pain in his face. But the girl's harsh reaction forbade me to even try a nonchalant glance his way.

"Oh, don't you dare! Don't you dare turn this around

and make me the bad guy."

Okay, I was weak. I couldn't help it. I had to catch a glimpse of what was to come. I inserted the correct key into the lock of my apartment door and peered out of the corner of my eye. She poked him in the chest. Repeatedly.

"Again, this is why you are a jerk. You think the world revolves around you and that you play no part in its destruction when it's crumbling around you. You're above it all, yet so far up its ass you can't see the light of day."

He didn't budge or even stop her finger-poke punishment. He stared at her, stunned. "I can't believe you didn't like the song. I was up all night. I wrote that for *you,* Caroline."

My eyes grew wide of their own volition. A songwriter? My sexy, half-dressed, James Tudor underwear model-like neighbor was a songwriter? My heart melted as I stood there. I imagined this man—yes…he was still sporting the towel—hunkered down over a well-worn set of piano keys, pounding out words of love and emotion with each lyrical stanza, every consecutive note inspired by the last. In my mind, I stood tall and proud, holding a white square sign with a bold, black, number ten on it above my head. Fireworks went off behind me in the distance, and a fluttering cloud of confetti fell around me.

This guy is a keeper!

I wanted to run up and give him a congratulatory hug on his big win, but the girlfriend—or soon-to-be-ex-girlfriend, if all of my assumptions were on the money—rolled her eyes and turned her back to him.

"You were never cut out to be a songwriter, Joseph. Just like you, your music lacks heart."

She left him standing in the narrow hallway, injured and bleeding. The knife in his chest remained at such a vicious angle that I began to wonder if he'd ever live through it. If it were me, I would have been crushed to the core. Then again, I wouldn't have settled for someone like her. I would have been smart enough to keep my standards raised and my heart better guarded.

Inwardly, I sighed. I supposed it was easier for me to say those things when I was outside looking in. I shouldn't have been listening in the first place. That's when my brain kicked into panic overdrive.

When he turned around, he'd see that I'd partaken in being a rude onlooker with a front row seat to his pathetic break-up. And I'd no longer be the cute, little neighbor who he—hypothetically speaking—might run into one day because he wasn't watching where he was going as he walked down the hall. He wouldn't suddenly feel compelled to ask me out on a date because he was a hopeless romantic and believed wholeheartedly in love at first sight. And fate.

Surely fate had a part in all this.

My mind raced as I continued to stand there like a deer in headlights, freaking out over the moment when he'd give up staring down the hall and turn toward his door. Before I could stop myself, I glanced down at the tiny rump hidden behind the stark-white terrycloth draped around his waist. I had all kinds of excuses for being the one who always gives into temptation, but considering the perilous situation I was in, I decided to save redemption for another day.

My terrycloth-kilted neighbor ran frustrated fingers through his dark, nigh-in-need-of-a-cut hair and, just as I feared, turned around.

I don't know who was more shocked, him or me. It was evident he hadn't expected to see anyone in the hall, much less a pale, brunette with barely a curve to her body, all of which were hidden behind a fluffy winter parka, scarf, and gloves.

I stared, frozen in my boots, my eyes bulging from their sockets. He returned the same stunned look. For a split second I thought I saw the corners of his mouth twitch upward in a smile. Of course, it might have been my overactive imagination on rapid-fire.

Short-lived as that thought was, his brow furrowed. He glanced back over his shoulder as if gathering his bearings on where he and his girlfriend had chosen to have their dispute and determining whether it were possible I witnessed it all from where I stood. I could have sworn I saw a hint of embarrassment on his face as he scratched his head. "Did you...I mean, did we disturb you? Could you actually hear us from inside?"

"Oh, no," I tried to explain at the same time I aimed to comfort him. "You didn't disturb me. I was out here the whole time—" I clamped my mouth shut. I had just blatantly admitted to eavesdropping on his personal conversation.

He eyes widened, and his chin tilted upward a bit. "Really..."

"I-I mean, not the whole time, just...well...."

It was my turn to be embarrassed, and I squeezed my eyes closed. Tightly. At least now, I could proudly say I was both weak and a horrible conversationalist.

Okay, you big idiot, say goodbye, cut your losses, and consider yourself lucky that he doesn't know your name. For all he knows, you're just a friend of the person who lives in Loft B and you were just leaving.

Better yet, perhaps he'll be so distraught over this whole morning that days from now when he runs into you again, as you're visiting your friend in Loft B, he won't even recognize you.

I liked the idea. So much that I'd already started plotting out my strategy. I'd donate this coat and the rest of my winter outerwear to Goodwill and buy a whole new ensemble, just in case he had a photographic memory. I'd act like we'd never met and start anew.

He came closer, his eyes zeroing in on me. They rivaled the bluest Montana sky on a summer afternoon. "You're the new girl?" he asked, pointing at me. "You just moved in a couple weeks ago. Sutherland, right?"

Wait. Did he just reveal in a very subtle, yet sly fashion that he took enough notice of me to remember my name? And how *did* he know my name? Had he broken into my mailbox and rummaged through my mail? Or worse, the dumpster?

No. I refused to believe this beautiful creature, as bold as he was talking to me in a towel, would resort to dumpster diving for any reason. Still, the question remained.

"Yeah, that's me. I'm Sutherland. Jamie Sutherland."

I had to look away. Joseph's eyes threatened to spellbind me, and I wondered how Caroline had the strength to deflect his hypnotic powers. By the looks of her glamorous appeal, I imagined she was a regular temptress herself, with the ability to stop traffic a mile away. I, on the other hand, was a plain Jane; brown hair, brown eyes, small build without a voluptuous curve in sight—the girl next door with the body of a twelve-year old boy—which was how a grudge-nursing ex-boyfriend once described me four years ago. To this day, I still choke up over his unpleasant portrayal.

"Welcome to the building, Jamie."

I dared to sneak another peek at him, hoping I could get through this conversation without looking like a faint-hearted schoolgirl. "How did you know my name?" I finally asked.

"Your name is on the mailbox for Loft B. I just put two and two together and came up with you."

It was nice to know the man knew his math. It should come in handy when he counted the reasons why he should've steered clear of me. Granted, I was not as needy as that Caroline girl, nor was I an attention-seeking drama queen. I avoided sinking to those emotional levels at all costs. I was a strong, independent woman who had no need for a man in her life. I'd tried the "couple" thing—multiple times—and I'd failed royally each go round.

Given the copious amounts of money I'd lost and the countless tears I'd shed over those "Mr. Rights" gone horribly wrong, I swore never to get sucked into the ridiculous notion of romance and all the frilly fringe benefits that supposedly came with it. I was a pessimistic woman. What I remembered most about love was not the endearing looks, warm hugs, or the cute butterflies in the stomach. It was the sucker punch in the gut when I least expected it.

"I should go," I said in haste, trying to remind myself that even this Greek Adonis-like man with kind blue eyes was capable of throwing a TKO punch.

He grinned, glanced down at his rather inappropriate attire, and thumbed over his shoulder toward his open apartment door. "Me too. Gotta get to work."

The innocence in his smile knocked me off balance. He went from bold and witty to downright adorable. It was a good thing he had already started to take a few steps backward, else I might have reached out and pinched his cute, five-o'clock-shadowed cheeks. The longer I stood here, the more I was convinced Caroline was clinically insane for going all diva on this man.

Stepping beneath his doorframe, he nodded once, reaffirming the beauty of his boyish grin, and closed the door.

A breath I had no idea I was even holding escaped me. My arms fell limp at my sides, keys rattling in my hand. I still had no grasp of what had really happened. The only thing that registered was Joseph and how he was quite possibly the best-looking jerk I'd ever seen.

Would you like to read the rest of

The Start of Something Good?

Visit **ReneeVincent.com** for your choice of print or ebook formats.

About Renee Vincent

RENEE VINCENT is a *USA Today* bestselling author of romance and women's fiction. Her books have earned numerous accolades, including a #1 Bestseller for Viking Romance.

She lives on a secluded hundred-acre horse farm in the rolling hills of Kentucky with her husband, two beautiful daughters, a couple of nocturnal dogs, and a pair of cats who think they're the masters of the house. Truth be told…they are.

www.ReneeVincent.com

Books By Series

Vikings of Honor Series
Sunset Fire, Book 1
Emerald Glory, Book 2
Souls Reborn, Book 3
Tempered Steel, Book 4

Mavericks of Meeteetse Series
Longing for Langston, Brody & Liv, Book 1
Made for McKinley, Jonas & Ava, Book 2
Falling For Forester, Cole & Crys, Book 3
Wild for Wallace, Sawyer & Charlotte, Book 4

Jamett & Joseph Series
The Start of Something Good, Book 1
The Road to Something Better, Book 2
The Gift of Something Grand, Book 3

Stand Alone Novel
Silent Partner

Mailing List

Sign up for Renee Vincent's author newsletter and reap the benefits of being one of her loyal subscribers! One lucky winner is drawn each month. What's more, you get a FREE BOOK just for joining.

Go to ReneeVincent.com, then click on "Newsletter" to sign up and start reading!

ReneeVincent.com